F Mortimer, Penelope, 1918-
   The handyman

NOV. 1985   12.95

the Handyman

the Handyman

PENELOPE MORTIMER

A
Joan
Kahn
BOOK

St. Martin's Press
New York

Library of Congress Cataloging in Publication Data

Mortimer, Penelope, 1918–
  The handyman.

  "A Joan Kahn book."
  I. Title.
PR6063.O815H3   1985   823'.914   85-11792
ISBN 0-312-35863-6

First published in Great Britain by Allen Lane, Penguin Books Ltd.

First U.S. Edition

10 9 8 7 6 5 4 3 2 1

the Handyman

Gerald Muspratt gave no indication of what he was about to do. He walked over to the french windows in the dining room to inspect the weather and, without even turning round, died. After he had done so – while he was doing it? – Phyllis ran from the end of the table, a long way to the empty window. The expression on his face was peaceful, his eyes and mouth shut and composed. He had even fallen quite neatly for an elderly man, one hand tucked under his cheek as though he were snoozing. But undeniably dead, gone for ever.

At first she trembled with shock, all of a dither; swivelled on her haunches, not knowing which way to turn, panting little gasps which sounded like oh dear, oh dear God, oh; her hands fluttered, patting, pulling at his hairy tweed jacket then flying away as though stung. She saw the table from an unknown angle, the packet of Bran Flakes blocking the ceiling, the heavy arches of the toast-rack tarnished on the inside, the shadow beneath the rim of the plate over which the dead man's marmalade oozed. What to do? Could he be left alone? She stumbled to her feet, took a few paces, looked back imploring him to stay there, blundered away again; and then, miraculously, the sound of the back door opening and slamming, the crash and puff of Mrs Rodburn's morning arrival.

Mrs Rodburn took over. By lunchtime Gerald had been removed, the table cleared, the breakfast things washed up and put away.

'Are you all right?' Sophia asked her mother, juggling with the vast problems this situation presented in terms of disruption of routine, not to mention guilt and – when there was time – grief.

'Yes, I'm all right,' Phyllis said shakily. 'It was his heart. I can't believe it yet, that's all.'

'Are *you* all right?' her son asked, the fervency of his voice unusual, for in fact he was crying, great tears running into his mouth, sopping his beard.

'Yes, I'm all right. It was his heart. I can't understand it yet, that's all.'

Michael croaked, 'He didn't do it on purpose,' not knowing what he was saying.

'Of course not,' she said, absolving Gerald, but not quite sure just the same. Her husband, her Gerald (she had loved him, after all), experiencing God knew what revelation, ecstasy or terror, in that moment when, his back turned to her, he had drawn his last breath; something entirely his own, infidelity at the last as he stepped off into air without so much as a glance in her direction.

She was bewildered and gave up trying to explain, even to herself. By the time the children arrived with furrowed faces and a few grey hairs, she had apparently settled for widowhood, suitably dressed and clutching a damp ball of paper tissue, willing to discuss the future and reminisce if necessary. Sophia, who felt that she herself had a quite unmerited attraction for responsibility, was relieved.

'She seems to be taking it very well,' she said to her brother. 'Thank God. I don't know about you, but I've got enough on my plate.'

Michael was suffering acutely. His father's death was the most momentous thing that had ever happened to him. It had happened only to him. His mother and sister were subsidiary ghosts. It was the night before the cremation and that afternoon they had all three gone to see – visit? – his father in his coffin. Sophia and her mother went into the room together, while he waited in the undertakers' dreadful vestibule. Sophia came out crying, but his mother had been curiously calm. The experience would be contained, he thought, in every conscious and unconscious moment of his future life. That travesty of a man he could have picked up with one hand, that effigy – had they stored the trunk for some ghastly purpose, leaving only the head and neck, the stiff yellow arms displayed on

6

satin? He hadn't dared to pry – worse, perhaps, to find the shrivelled bundle of penis and testicles than nothing at all. He couldn't understand ·vhat Sophia was saying. He was distraught.

'I couldn't make up my mind whether to bring Jasper,' Sophia went on relentlessly. She felt a great need to talk to someone. She was used to the need, but usually suppressed it. It was unjust that when she actually wanted to talk about something other than the state of her marriage, her husband wasn't there to listen. She had never really talked to Michael. He was her older brother, she was fond of him, but she didn't know anything about him. It was the kind of family in which the sexes paired off. She realized, dimly, that Michael felt lonelier than she did, particularly since he didn't have a family of his own, but she had no idea of the arctic wastes of his loneliness. 'But he's only three, after all, so we thought it better not. Bron's awfully sorry – he was very fond of Daddy and I wish he could have been here, I mean he wishes it too, but it seemed better for him to stay behind with Jasper, though *I* don't know, perhaps we were wrong . . .'

Her voice fell like rain. From time to time he looked up to see whether it had stopped. 'Anyway, she'll be all right for money. This house must be worth a packet. She'll sell it, of course – I do think she must, don't you? It's a dreadful old place really but it must be worth at least a hundred grand, being where it is. Do you remember that time he took us to Whipsnade . . . it was Whipsnade wasn't it? . . .'

No, Michael didn't remember. He remembered only that thing in the coffin. He thought he was shouldering the whole burden of death, and it crushed him.

Phyllis wouldn't have called herself an imaginative woman, but her love for her son made her ingenious. She found herself devising a kind of formal dance, approach and retreat, circle and curtsey, which she hoped might make him feel in charge while at the same time relieving him of all responsibility. So, apparently submissive, she asked him to make arrangements which were inevitable; she granted him filial obligations and, with a graceful chassé, withdrew anxiety. He performed instinctively, without knowing it, in a dream, stooping and shambling. He wore a black tie at the cremation, an exclamation point of grief on an otherwise non-committal shirt. Phyllis longed to take his hand, but leant on him instead, as seemed proper.

To his dear wife, Phyllis Ellen Muspratt, Gerald had left everything, except for meticulously detailed bequests to the two children, his son-in-law Bron, his grandson, and any future grandchildren he might have up to a total of six. Michael was not singled out. Indeed, lacking a family, he received rather less than Sophia. It appeared that Gerald had not known how much his son cared for him; or if he had, it was not something to be specially rewarded. A retired bank manager, even a careful one, doesn't have a great deal to leave, and no sentiments were expressed in the Will. His binoculars went to young Jasper, presumably for bird-watching.

*

For a couple of months Phyllis was treated like an invalid, which both irritated and consoled her. Then everyone returned to their own lives, uneasily wondering how to fit her in. Sophia's and Michael's visits became less frequent. Friends, now outnumbering her two to one, worded their invitations differently. Instead of being asked to dinner, she was invited to 'supper – just family – any time'. If she went, there was a kind of lethargy about the cauliflower cheese and the supermarket Riesling, often already opened. Weekending children, mainly middle-aged, discussed mutual acquaintances with their parents; married couples slipped easily into conversations they would have had if they were by themselves, snapping at each other, revealing prejudices and opinions Phyllis had never been aware they held, often upsetting. Towards the first Christmas there were more formal gatherings, Sunday morning sherry and mid-week dinner parties where, to her horror, she found herself paired with some unattached man whom her hosts hardly knew, some enigma or variation discovered lurking in an address book like a spare denture. She had nothing, she felt, to offer these people, and social occasions without Gerald for anchor were agony for her. The best thing was to stay at home and try to preserve her dignity. She had never considered dignity before. It appealed to her.

'Are you thinking of moving?' she was asked.

'Moving? Oh no, I don't think so. I know where I am here.'

But perhaps that wasn't true. She began to read the Property Columns, tutting softly to herself at the prices people asked and would, presumably, pay. Her bills for rates and fuel and electricity were shocking – Gerald had always said they were, and she had always sympathized, but she had never actually seen them before. It began to seem indecent to spend so much money just on herself.

'All I really need is a small flat somewhere.'

'Not in London,' Sophia said, sounding oppressed.

'Oh, no.' She had in fact thought of London, but speculated wildly, 'Hove, perhaps.'

'You'd go crazy in Hove,' Sophia said. She was pregnant, and the idea of her mother living in a flat in Hove seemed, illogically, the final treachery. 'What would you *do* in Hove?'

'I don't know,' Phyllis said, thinking about it for a moment, until it became unpleasant.

Sophia's pregnancy took her mind off her mother's problems; she reluctantly agreed to send Jasper to stay while she was having the baby, pinning a list of instructions to his pyjamas, where it couldn't be missed. For the first time since Gerald's death, Phyllis knew what was required of her; she treated her grandson exactly as she had treated Gerald, with love and concern and mild exasperation. He was homesick and disgruntled to begin with, but soon continued to educate her in the habits of Great Tits and Tree Pipits. She mentioned on the phone that he had cried a little the first night, and Bron came the following day and took him home. 'We don't want

9

him to hold it against Selina,' he said. 'These things can be pretty dodgy, you know.'

Confronting loneliness was bad enough; now Phyllis felt humiliated and incompetent. The house didn't accommodate her or adapt to her needs; it wanted Gerald. She put it on the market for a few weeks, but took it off again after unpleasant couples had kicked the drainpipes and sneered at the radiators. She was alarmed to find how inconsistent she was becoming – or had always been?

Feeling it might be stabilizing, she tried to spend more time in the garden, though she was too timid to do much more than dead-head the roses and pull out the weeds she recognized. Gerald was an upsetting presence. The trouble was she couldn't hear what he said. Time we got what in? Do what to the syringa? He had always been so busy, coming and going with the ladder and the pruning hook, spraying, planting, piling up the wheelbarrow, measuring out strange chemicals, never coming in to wash his hands until at least ten minutes after she had called him. She knew he thought – would have thought – her pottering desultory and aimless. Mr Rodburn now came to mow the grass and clip the hedges, but he was a mechanic by trade and useless without machinery. He suggested she bought a cultivator and a weed-eater and an electric hoe, and when these failed to appear he spent longer and longer in the garage stripping down the mower and oiling the hedge-cutter with black rags. She couldn't afford to offend the Rodburns, but she didn't know if she could afford to keep them either. Vague dilemmas shadowed her nights. She didn't speak of them, afraid to be seen not to be managing her life.

*

In order to see her children, she now made brief visits to London as Sophia's guest.

'Do you remember Emma Thwaite? She was at school with me – came to stay once.'

'No ... Or was she that clever, plain one?' Phyllis was

drying the dishes, a task which Sophia had pointed out was unnecessary. The children were in bed, Bron not home yet. Phyllis relished these rare moments alone with her daughter, enjoying gossip.

'She may have been clever then,' Sophia said doubtfully, rinsing a cup her mother had just dried and putting it on the plate-rack. 'Not any more. She married someone called Jack Sanderson. Anyway, Bron met them somewhere and they said they wanted to sell their cottage, so he asked them round. Thinking of you, of course.'

'How kind,' Phyllis said, without enthusiasm.

'It sounds as though it might be just the thing.'

'Really. Why?'

'Well, it's small, and it's got a garden and it's in a village and it's easy to get to. They bought it from his aunt – maybe that's why they don't want to do it through an estate agent or anything, in case she's offended. I don't know. I said we might go and see it on Saturday.'

'Oh, I can't possibly go on Saturday. I've got to get home, darling. Still, it was a nice thought.' She looked busily for some distraction. 'Shall I lay the table?'

'That's too bad, because I've told Bron he's got to look after the kids, and they're expecting us for lunch. Never mind.' Sophia sighed deeply, and looked worn. 'I just felt I could do with an outing.'

*

'Sophia's taking me off tomorrow to see some cottage she's found,' Phyllis said importantly. 'She thinks I ought to move.'

'Move?' Michael asked, his fine eyes doubting her. 'Why?'

They were lunching in the restaurant where Michael entertained – rather lugubriously, she imagined – his authors. It had pleased her that the waiters treated him with such respectful familiarity and that grown men, many of them portly and balding, were careful to salute him. She had been glad that she had worn the grey suit, a tailored complement to her soft grey hair, and that she still had a figure of sorts and didn't feel her appearance unseemly in such a place. It had made her careless. Now, typically, she hesitated, anxious not to upset him, then made do with what seemed to her a vague summary – the house too big, too expensive, the rates alone . . . With each fact Michael flinched, as though she were applying iodine to a grazed knee, although it was his conscience that hurt. He did not wish to know about selling and buying, disposing of furniture, registers, deeds, charges, the duties of death. His mother wasn't asking anything of him, but he wanted to tell her angrily to ask Sophia, whose son had inherited the binoculars. 'Of course I shan't buy this place,' she said. 'Between you and me, I'm only going so that Sophia can have a day off. But it's true,' – she looked away from him, smoothing the tablecloth – 'perhaps I do need a change . . .'

Fogged with trouble, he glared at her without seeing. Wasn't death enough change for her? It must have been virgin sperm that had travelled through that old womb; an immaculate progeniture, like everything else the old man did. 'Of course,' he mumbled. 'I suppose so. Well, if there's anything I can do . . .'

She knew he didn't mean it but for an instant, stretching her love to include them both, allowed herself to be reassured. My son will deal with that, my son would never allow it, I must ask my son. Well, never mind. She twitched the intangible membrane back, briskly folded it, tucked it away.

'Thank you, darling.' But the rejection made her cruel. 'You know – we lived together for forty-five years.' Now she had all his attention. 'I never really thought of us being separate people. Perhaps you can believe he's dead, but I can't. I'm looking for him all the time. Aren't I absurd?'

He signed the bill and hunched away from her, muttering something about the coffin.

'I don't care about what we saw in the coffin,' Phyllis said calmly. 'That wasn't Gerald. You mustn't think of that as Gerald.'

So, having enraged her son, she left him, feeling a greater sense of mourning than she had so far felt for her husband. She no longer knew what her role was, pulled this way and that, protected and unprotected, assumed to be dependent on those who ought to depend on her and independent by those who didn't know how to treat her as a solitary woman. In the meanwhile, she would let Sophia think she was doing something positive.

*

The journey seemed all too quick while they were on the motorway. Phyllis was entertained by Sophia's absurd suggestions.

'Perhaps you'll get married again.'

'Don't be ridiculous, darling!'

'Why not? It's your profession. I mean, you're good at it.'

'Then I've retired.'

'I don't believe it. It's funny how some people are natural wives and some people' – she sounded momentarily dejected – 'are just women.'

That was the nearest they came to what Phyllis thought of as 'a real talk', but it gave her confidence. Maybe it really was possible to start a new life. Once they had turned off the motorway she commented happily on the countryside, as though they were abroad, comparing it very favourably with Surrey. But when they left the main road and began following Emma's instructions, winding through single-track lanes, peering for landmarks, she began to be more critical.

'"Sharp left by slum at top of hill",' she read. '"*Slum*"?' Then they saw it, a shanty town sprawling into the woods, overflowing dustbins and a group of meagre children kicking a football. 'I don't like the look of *that*,' she said, with satisfaction. 'And it must be part of the village because it says here "Cryck, 200 yards down the hill".' She gave this eyesore more elaborate attention than she had given any manor house, ancient church or natural view, turning round to see the last of it through the rear window. 'I'm surprised they allow such places. It can't be good for the neighbourhood.'

But she had to admit that the village, though it seemed curiously deserted, was charming, and Coachman's Cottage – 'cottage' had led her to expect half-timbered gables and mice – a sturdy little house, quite dignified in its way apart from the dreadful metal swing and plastic sand-pit in the front garden. The Sandersons, a pleasant, distraught young couple, offered sherry and crisps. The children had gone to their grandmother for the weekend, a blessing. 'I'd love to be able to send mine to Mother more often,' Sophia said, 'but she has such a huge house and no proper help, it's really too much for her.' An outrageous lie. Phyllis retaliated by asking who owned that disgraceful place at the top of the hill, it looked most insanitary. It was where the Brigadier's workmen lived, they said. Brigadier 'Ricky' Wainwright, quite a character. He owned the farm too. In fact he owned almost everything round here, except this cottage. They'd bought this from Aunt Pip, who lived at the Old Rectory.

'She'd love it if you came here,' Emma said. 'She's such a sweet person. You'd get on terribly well.'

'And there's Rebecca,' Jack said. 'Very good value, Rebecca.'

'He means Rebecca Broune – o-u-n-e – the writer. You've probably heard of her. She's a bit unpredictable, but *we* like her, don't we, Jack?'

Sophia, having already made up her mind that this was where her mother should live, asked if they could look round the house. Emma led the way, starting with the attic ('Lovely nursery,' Sophia said carelessly), warning Phyllis of the steep, twisting staircase (what does she think I am? Decrepit?), saying they really would have done something about the bathroom if they had been staying. Phyllis, thinking it a crime that such a pretty house should be so neglected, was a little brusque. 'Your husband isn't a handyman, obviously. I suppose he doesn't have the time.' Gerald wouldn't have put up

14

with that bathroom for a minute. Neither would she. How busy they could have been, the two of them. She was careful not to show her interest, but by the time they sat down to lunch she had already redecorated and furnished the place in her mind's eye while her own, downcast, observed the ham and lettuce with distaste.

Jack was doing his best to sell, no doubt of it. Cryck was a perfect place to live – or would be, for the right person. They were so anxious to find the right person that they hadn't put the house on the open market, they preferred to sell to a friend. And we do think of Aunt Pip, of course. For anyone who didn't have to commute, or didn't have children coming up to school-age – well, for an elderly widow for instance, it would be just the thing – Lamberts Heath so near, milk and eggs delivered from Tyler Farm, a reliable gardener – Bill Slattery, he worked for Aunt Pip, came to them on Saturdays. Was Phyllis a keen gardener? Jack suspected she was. Emma was very good at herbs.

Phyllis didn't feel that any of this concerned her. It was the house that appealed, for rescue as much as anything else, like an abandoned cat or child. Jack insisted on taking her outside while Emma and Sophia washed up. 'Wonderful position, isn't it? Aunt Pip's a bit pushed for money since Uncle died, she just sold her last 500 acres to keep the horses, she couldn't live without those. I bought a bit of it – you see that field going down to the river? Thought we might build on to the house, but the Planning people turned me down. You could make a pretty good vegetable garden there. Or a tennis court. Ideal place for a swimming pool, too.'

He seemed to be talking at random. To relieve him, Phyllis said she would wander round by herself. She was trying to imagine what it would be like to live in such an unfamiliar, westerly place without rhododendrons or azaleas, Sainsbury's or a Green Line bus. Without Gerald. Well, never altogether without Gerald, but it was time she stopped believing that he was going to come back, waiting for something that could never happen. The dead Gerald, the memory, might enjoy it here; he might not – well, haunt her so much. New friends would perhaps treat her as an independent old woman instead of some sort of left-over from their middle age. The Brigadier might have a wife, Mrs Chalmers sounded very pleasant, the Vicar would call. It had been a little difficult in Surrey since the war, people moved in and out and the town had stopped being what you might call a community; even so, if anyone obviously permanent bought one of the older houses, she would always pop round with her card and a friendly wel-come. One might have a small sherry party perhaps or, if the newcomer were a single woman like Lady Brabington or Miss Skeffington-Nodes, coffee. It didn't always lead anywhere, but it was well meant. In the 'real' country – she did realize Surrey wasn't that any more – she believed these old customs still survived. Then of course the villagers would be helpful – there would be cheery Good-days, advice, even confidences. She was sure she could make the best marmalade, the lightest sponge cakes; perhaps she might even be asked to join the Parish Council. It was time she started taking an interest in such things, time she was useful.

She was busy with these thoughts as she walked down the overgrown paths, ducking under branches heavy with rotting plums, noticing neglected roses, dahlias, red-hot pokers which momentarily reminded her of home and Gerald, who hadn't liked them. She walked down to the stream – absurd to call it a river – across the newly acquired field, unmown and ungrazed for many years, pitted with mole hills, uncompromisingly square inside a chicken-wire fence. Who-ever bought the place would have to put up a proper fence. She must find out who owned the land on either side – they could probably come to some arrangement. The cottage looked pretty as a picture, its sunny face turned towards her, the grey village straggling up behind it flanked by autumn gold and crimson, topped by stately clouds hanging in a blue sky.

The Sandersons had improved their tactics by the time she got back. Sophia was looking worried.

'We do love it here, you know,' Emma said. 'We can't bear the thought of leaving.'

'In fact we've by no means made up our minds,' Jack said. 'I do hope you realize that, Mrs Muspratt.'

Phyllis enjoyed Bridge and Poker, played Snap like lightning and always cleared the Scrabble board. She was a good winner, gracious in triumph. 'I'm very happy in Surrey,' she smiled. 'This was entirely Sophia's idea. I'm afraid it's not my part of the world at all.'

'You mean you won't even consider it?' Sophia asked as they waved good-bye to the doleful couple at the gate.

'Of course I will. I already have. But I'm not going to pay their price, my dear. Just look at that bathroom.'

The decision in her voice was alarming. Sophia herself always tried to work things out, weighing the pros and cons. She thought the place was ideal, but surely a long discussion was called for?

'You mustn't be hasty,' she said uneasily. 'I mean – it's a big step. You need to be quite certain.'

'Oh, I'm quite certain.' Phyllis settled herself for a short nap. She was amazed to find how easy it was to take decisions. 'It seems such a pity,' she said, her eyes gently closing, 'to leave all those plums to the wasps . . .'

Phyllis had lived with her parents, first in Married Quarters and then in Haywards Heath, until – barely more than a schoolgirl, she said – she had married Gerald. Objects, even rooms, had been considered her own, but of course they weren't. There had always been some alternative arrangement, someone else to consider. Perhaps this was why she had kept most of her clothes, the only things she had chosen entirely for herself (or was that true? She had dressed, and still did, as an officer's daughter and bank manager's wife). There was no space in the cupboard for half of them, so she hung the good evening dresses and town suits in the attic. Up and down the narrow stairs, uncertain of her footing in the dark, not yet knowing where to find light switches. They'd never get a coffin down here, surely. Preparing for visitors? Preparing for what?

Neither of the children had wanted any furniture, so most of it had been auctioned. The chintz-covered armchairs and sofas, the dining table and sideboards and dressing tables had all gone; so had the water-colours and prints, the works of John Buchan, the decanters and cruets and canisters that had seemed so necessary thirty, forty years ago. Gerald's heavy tools, his collection of *National Geographics* and his fishing rods had been disposed of by Sophia, who knew that her mother would find them hard to part with. Phyllis didn't exactly miss it all, but she felt sparse. She wasn't sure that it was suitable for a widow of her age to have no accumulation of useless objects. She wasn't sure what she meant by suitable.

It was now two and a half years since Gerald's death; she didn't think about him quite so often. Still, when she did, sitting outside her back door those first spring evenings in Cryck, or wandering down to the stream to look at the cows and minnows, she knew that the preparations and the sense of sparseness both came from her morbid conviction that he was going to come back. She couldn't even bring herself to find someone to fix up the bathroom, let alone deal with the draughts and the wiring. It was the same with the garden. Silly, she knew, but to interfere in such things made her feel disloyal. She would wait a little longer, there was no reason to rush into things.

She waited for two weeks, then three. Everything was unpacked, the floors scrubbed, the walls washed, the windows cleaned. The reliable gardener didn't turn up. Nobody came near her, not even somebody organizing a Jumble Sale, collecting for Save the Children, selling Lifeboat pins. She had expected Mrs Chalmers, at least – and where was the Vicar? She very seldom saw anyone when she walked up the village, except for a few rough young men who didn't somehow look as though they belonged. Perhaps they came from that slum in the woods. They made her uncomfortable; they hit the cowparsley with sticks as they slouched by; at night there were motor bikes tearing up the hill, sometimes a blaring burst of music in the dark. She asked the postman who they were but he just shook his head, as though she had been imagining things.

She didn't want to impose on Mrs Chalmers – not yet, anyway – and told herself that it was no good expecting the Vicar to take an interest in her if she didn't go to church, though she couldn't feel that was the right, Christian way to look at it. So on her third Sunday she powdered her nose and, since it was a chilly day, put on her fur coat (the good old Beaver) and walked up the overgrown track to the church to find that there was no service in Cryck until the following Sunday, and then only Holy Communion. She had nothing against Holy Communion, except that to tell herself the truth she found the thought of body and blood a little repugnant before breakfast; but she liked the friendliness of Matins, or whatever they called it nowadays, and was disappointed. The inner door of the church was locked – there must be a reason, she was sure it was against some law – so she walked round the churchyard, and peered at a few tombstones, which told her little except that the expectation of life in Cryck was short. It was quite encouraging to see a new grave; at least someone had recently had a funeral – and well-attended, if the flowers were anything to go by. She put on her glasses to read the smudged tags: 'To Pippa, with love always', 'To Aunt Pip, a great lady', 'To Granny P. with lots of love, we miss you', 'To Mrs Chalmers, with respectful sorrow . . .'

Mrs Chalmers? Aunt Pip? Dead? Why hadn't someone told her? It explained, of course, why she hadn't called (would never call), but how extraordinary of the Sandersons not to let her know. It was a shock. From one minute to the next, her sense of pleasurable anticipation – for Mrs Chalmers, like Gerald, had been alive, could have come to the door one day, telephoned, come up to her in the street any time – was extinguished. She had tried telling herself very often that death meant 'never again'. It hadn't convinced her. Now it was starkly 'never', and that did.

She realized that she was trembling as she turned over the tags. There was no 'again'. It was just 'never'. Hard to grasp, but she had already accepted it. Like swimming, when she couldn't swim; jumping from a high building, when she couldn't stand heights. You were suddenly doing it, though you didn't know how. 'Regrets – Brigadier Wainwright and all at Tyler House', 'Pippa passes – J W', 'Mrs Philippa Chalmers – in gratitude to a true friend – F. Skerry', 'She took the last fence – in fond memory, Harry and Jane', 'For darling Auntie Pip – Jack and Emma, Sebastian and Midge'. 'Well!' Phyllis said out loud. She took off her glasses and hurried back through the churchyard. She had come into it thinking that something pleasant and comforting was going to happen. She went out of it knowing for the first time that Gerald was dead.

It was hard to believe that this was progress. For the first few days she panicked, scuttled about the cottage whimpering, distraught. She had been counting on Mrs Chalmers; she had been counting on Gerald. What was she doing in this strange place? She couldn't remember why she had come. Perhaps she should go back to Surrey – no, that would be defeat. But what was she going to do with the rest of her life, day, the next ten minutes? There was no one to ask. She could telephone Sophia, but Sophia would either be fetching Jasper from school or putting Selina to bed or distracted with some crisis. She could telephone Michael, but he would be at the office, or out, or busy, and it would only upset him. She could write to some of those good friends she had criticized so harshly, friends of Gerald's, but what should she say? Anyway – this was Thursday, she was calming down – she hadn't got any stamps. She could go into Lamberts Heath and buy some stamps – a firm decision until she remembered it was early closing, and even in her desperation she couldn't justify driving all that way just to go to the post office. She could make soup from that wilting watercress. She could watch television – no, never in daylight, unless it was tennis. She wondered if it was blasphemous to wish that this cup could be taken from her; it might be small compared with some, but it tasted bitter.

But Phyllis was the product of generations bred in kindly optimism and small expectation; she wasn't aware of it, but she was supported. The Muspratts might admit to passing over or beyond or away, they might lose each other or even be deceased but they never said die. Grasp the nettle firmly, they told her. Pull yourself together. Heaven helps those who help themselves. She drove into Lamberts Heath on Monday determined to find something to belong to, something to join. There were no more Geralds in the world, of course, but there must be another Mrs Chalmers somewhere, interested in Roman history, perhaps, or the theatre, or even folk-lore.

Lamberts Heath puzzled her. Everyone had been perfectly civil until she had said she lived in Cryck; then (it must be her imagination), they seemed to slam down shutters, bolt doors.

'I'd like to open an account,' she had said to the butcher.

'Yes, madam. Certainly, madam. You've just moved here, I take it?' Friendly, respectful, anxious for her custom.

'Mrs Muspratt is the name – Coachman's Cottage, Cryck.'

It hadn't been her imagination – his pencil paused, then he scribbled illegibly and looked over her head at the next customer. 'Yes, Mrs Robinson – what can we do for you today?' Dismissed. Rejected. Unrecognized. She hadn't even given her order – not that it was really worth it for two lamb chops. She now did all her shopping in the supermarket and paid cash, which was horribly impersonal. Mrs Chalmers might have been able to explain. Oh bother Mrs Chalmers. This must be progress.

The library was the answer. She went bustling in to find something to belong to, join, take part in, but apart from a poster announcing a Bring and Buy Sale there was no such information in the lobby. She couldn't believe this and addressed herself to one of the librarians behind the desk. 'Good morning – my name is Mrs Muspratt and I've recently moved here. I wonder if you could tell me of any local societies – groups, you know, and so on – I might join? Or I expect you have a programme of lectures here at the library, or perhaps at the Town Hall – ?'

The woman looked quite friendly. 'There's the Women's Institute ...'

'Yes, of course, but I was thinking of something a little more ...' She smiled pinkly, in confidence. 'After all, I do *know* how to arrange flowers and make jam tarts, you see. I was thinking more of a Music Society or a drama group or an Historical Society ... Well, you know the sort of thing?'

'We don't have anything like that,' the woman said. 'Do we, Doris?'

Doris said firmly, 'Oh, no. We don't have anything like that.'

It was too bad. 'I'll join the library, anyway.' She filled in the form and handed it back. 'Perhaps I'll try and tackle Henry James – he seems to come over very well on television, don't you think?'

The woman read the entry on the form and passed it to Doris, who sniffed. 'Cryck,' she said.

'We don't have Henry James on the shelves,' the woman said. 'There's no call for him.'

Phyllis was extremely put out. She even indicated that Lamberts Heath, compared with Surrey, appeared to be at a low intellectual ebb and that she might well make a report to the County Librarian. Of course they *had* Henry James, the woman said, it was just that they didn't *display* Henry James, there being no call for him, but if you could *wait* a few minutes Henry James might well be found in the store room. Feeling that she had made her mark, Phyllis sat down to wait by Reference. To pass the time she looked through last year's *Who's Who*, not that she knew anyone who was likely to be in it – unless perhaps the writer, Rebecca Broune, not Brown, who lived in Cryck? And there indeed she was.

Broune, Rebecca Pamela, FRSL, writer, *d* of Leonard Albert Williams & Eleanor Mary Williams, *m* 1st David Letherway 1936 (*diss* 1941), *m* 2nd Andrew Philip Broune 1941 (*diss* 1945), 1 *d*, *m* 3rd Ralph Daniel Herbert 1948 (*diss* 1968, 1 *s*, 1 *d*. Hon. Mem. Amer. Academy of Arts & Letters, Mem. Inst. for Cultural Res. Education: The Old Barn, Liss, Hants. Publications . . .

Well, the publications were to be expected, and there were certainly a lot of them, but three husbands, and all still alive as far as one knew, that was surely a little excessive? Three children, though, and since she and Mrs Broune were of an age they might possibly have something in common – even grandchildren. Her fantasy soared for a moment, inspired by loneliness and the room of tired books. Supposing this was fate's reason for sending her to Cryck? A friend, far cleverer, of course, than people like Mrs Chalmers and herself, and busy with her work, but she would certainly know everyone worth knowing – 'Very good value, Rebecca,' Jack Sanderson had said. Now why had she forgotten that? She could hardly change her mind about Henry James, having made such a fuss, but she would certainly take Rebecca Broune's books out next time. Loaded with *The Ambassadors*, *The Golden Bowl* and *The Sacred Flame*, all disinterred from the store room where they had apparently mouldered for eight years, Phyllis drove home full of purpose. If Mahomet wouldn't come to the mountain, the mountain – the image even made her smile – must pull its socks up. She would call on Rebecca Broune.

Although a few months younger than Phyllis, Rebecca Broune had lived much longer and in a very different way. The only child of a progressive schoolmaster and a hospital nurse – progressivism in the twenties had much to do with looms and bowels – she had been encouraged to leave her father's school, which was also her home, at the age of fifteen, and had been unable to find a satisfactory substitute until she was well over fifty. Her three marriages and countless love affairs had all ended in disaster; so, on numerous occasions, had she herself, or very nearly, snatched back by stomach-pumps, blood transfusions, electric current, medication of the most dubious kind and enough psychiatrists to set up a small symposium. All this had not made her the happiest of women, but had given her insight of a kind. She was adept at finding the Achilles heel, the soft underbelly, the mask behind the face. The world – or that small part of the world which she had briefly agitated – suffered from this and kept away.

So, if forced to it, Rebecca might have described herself. She would have described her appearance with equal relish, admitting that she had been beautiful up to middle age, without knowing it; that now she was ugly, and did. Her ugliness gave her a curious satisfaction. It protected her against upstarts and repelled nuisances. In case anyone should see through it she reinforced it with wild, greying hair, baggy denim, shapeless clod-hopping shoes; what remained of her fingernails were ridged with earth; through constantly holding a cigarette in the corner of her mouth, one eye had become smaller and redder than the other. Her appearance was a challenge which nowadays few people were curious enough to accept.

Apart from her three children – who seemed to have inherited nothing from her and therefore didn't count – she was the last in a long line of dilettantes, rolling stones and failures; the distaff side had provided money, respectability, and harshness of spirit. So Eleanor Mary, the hospital nurse, had inherited money from her grandmother, an heiress to panama hats, and Leonard Albert, the progressive schoolmaster, had inherited the balance of his mother's fortune after her husband had squandered a great deal of it on futile enterprises. With this capital they had started The Old Barn Co-educational School, vaguely run according to the principles of A. S. Neill and their neighbour Dora Russell. Leonard knew very little about these principles and was too lazy to find out. Eleanor fervently devoted herself to nuts and raw carrot, encouraging every tendency to self-immolation in her goose-pimpled, gibbering charges. Most of these children were castaways from wealthy homes, all unloved, many delinquent. Some of them stayed during the holidays, as a convenience to their parents. For over ten years they were Rebecca's sole companions.

Although Leonard and Eleanor insisted that there was no favouritism, Rebecca was nevertheless daughter of the house and gave the others a bad time. Her average intelligence, compared with theirs, was genius; her natural intellectual greed was fed on anaemic folk-lore, the study of catkins and the more easily assimilated thoughts of Nietzsche; she learned to play the recorder and to weave rough yarn in ethnic patterns. Unlike the other children, she read everything in the house – Pearl Buck, Mary Webb, Arnold Bennett, Galsworthy – but knew nothing of Shakespeare or the Bible. In her adolescence she wrote quantities of poetry inspired by Alfred Noyes, Browning and Longfellow, and was told by her father, an impractical man, that she might become a writer some day; since she couldn't dance or paint or even play the recorder with any skill, he couldn't think of any alternative. Eleanor, made of sterner stuff, decided on early marriage as the only possible occupation for her aimless girl, though she had omitted telling her any facts about it, or even how to boil an egg.

In the meanwhile, since Rebecca showed no inclination for nursing, she should train as a shorthand-typist.

The shock of the mental discipline that this involved pitched Rebecca into the first arms that offered refuge, which were those of an elderly actor in the local repertory company. At the age of eighteen she published her first novel, the story of an affair between a young girl and an elderly actor in a local repertory company. It was a simple, savage little work which, in the sentimental but uneasy climate of the 1930s, won considerable notoriety. She married a younger, more successful actor, to whom she was frequently unfaithful, finding monogamy unconducive to ideas. By the age of thirty, assisted by two divorces, enormous energy and arrogance and the Second World War, she was an established literary figure, clever enough to pull the wool over the eyes of many serious critics, naïve enough to pluck the public's heart-strings. With her third husband, a cultured Jewish banker, she settled down to what promised to be a relatively quiet, affluent life, conducive to work and perhaps, at last, to education.

Both were against her nature. For a while Isabel, whom she had taken with her into the Herbert stronghold, was a minor distraction; then it was the Herbert heir, and after that another girl. Only three years of her life had been spent in pregnancy – apart from the time wasted in her youth on abortions and general upsets associated with being a woman – but while the experience might be useful, she resented it. Instead of staying at home, quietly esteemed, she went off and spent arduous months in New Jersey and Iowa lecturing to gullible, though intellectually superior, American graduates. She was worshipped in Massachusetts, degraded in California. She wrote film scripts of her novels, wearily rehashing exhausted emotions; those that still troubled her were bewildering and seemed irrelevant to her life. She might have got by if her brain had been more adequately equipped, but the recorder and Arnold Bennett failed her and her talent, overexploited and under-nourished, ran thin. Unable to lie fallow and take stock – these were the years when boredom nearly killed her – she accepted every invitation to appear on panels and forums, to be quizzed and questioned. Her public statements became increasingly irrational. Rebecca had never fooled herself, but her image at least had been reliable. Now, beyond her control, it collapsed, stumbled up again, desperately tried to keep going. In a final effort to destroy it, and at the same time keep herself alive, Rebecca ended her marriage on a trivial pretext – Priscilla her name was, a bright girl – and bought a remote cottage off a stranger in a Bayswater pub. He was the last soggy chip off some family tree, but she didn't inquire further. Six months later she moved in with a suitcase, never having seen the place.

It was almost a year before the telephone stopped ringing and the unanswered letter-writers lost patience. During that time Rebecca hid, living like a hermit, feigning dead. Then one spring morning, with great caution and little curiosity, she went out of doors.

It seemed she owned nearly two acres, a sizable patch of the earth's surface. Finding some rusty tools in an outhouse, she began to slash and uproot the undergrowth. It was the most pleasurable thing she had done for years. She began to dig, more or less at random; she dammed the stream, made a living pool, built a wall from the excavated stone. She came across an obscure Edwardian writer who suggested that what she felt was 'a vague discontent with the earth as it is . . . a yearning for the companionship of beautiful and dependent things . . . a need to find vent for emotions which one is unwilling to express to one's fellows'. There was the delight, after years of searching for tortuous motives and intellectual excuses, of finding how simple her needs actually were, though 'vague discontent' was too mild for her. Through one good eye and perpetual smoke she saw shapes, colours and perspectives in her wilderness and heaved, dug, planted and plotted until they began to emerge; then it was all wrong and with furious impatience she tore it up, shoved everything round until, temporarily, she was satisfied. Her achievements in those first five years were not due to chance or to some personal, insignificant talent, as she felt her writing to be; they resulted from natural arrogance and energy, with the co-operation of living things. And money.

Bloody money was essential. She was haunted by time wasted, lack of time. Her couple of acres must be forced into maturity in a few years if she was to see the results before she died. She had never thought about the future; never really believed in it. Now she discovered that as well as owing her publishers a large advance for a book that would never be written, her royalties were negligible, her capital gone. Ralph, her last husband, gave her a small stipend for reasons which they had both forgotten, but it barely covered the rates and taxes; what she insisted on calling her Old Age Pension disappeared in heat, light, licences and – occasionally and sparsely – food. She found all this painful and irritating, but now she had a dependant it had to be faced. Swallowing her humiliation and rage, though never digesting them, she picked up the telephone again and touted for work, any work, the easier the better so long as it paid. She resented every hour thrown away on such stuff and gone for ever; she would not only have bitten the hands that fed her, but horribly mauled them if she could. She made it a point of honour to spend every cheque within twelve hours of receiving it – first a carton of cigarettes, then a litre or two of supermarket wine, then, with satisfaction that amounted at times to ecstasy, the garden. What would happen when she could no longer find any work was one of the questions that troubled her only on winter nights, when she was vulnerable to such things. In the present, which fortunately it usually was, her body was satisfied with hard labour and her mind becoming slowly accustomed to the study of plants. Her capacity for love, so misused and wasted over the years, was invested in roses.

No one who did not share this passion could know the tenderness, almost amounting to anguish, that old roses disturbed in Rebecca Broune's wary heart. During her long working life she had written volumes on the variations of love, but the fragile survivors of Egypt and Pompeii, the damasks of Paestum, the Renaissance Albas and Bourbons from the Indian Ocean and wild briars of ancient China, the blood of Christ and the purity of Mary – neither of whom she found significant in any other way – silenced her. This silence was the nearest approach to the state of what other people called happiness that she had ever known. If she had been asked to explain her life – and thank God, she wasn't – she would have kept quiet about the winter questioning, the obscure discomforts of the dark, and modestly admitted that she was better off than she had any right to be, considering her history.

Her children were connected with the bad years; she seldom thought about them, although Isabel occasionally wrote stilted, unhappy letters, not at all interesting. As for friends, though many people had been in love with Rebecca, very few of them had liked her. She was distant with talented or intelligent people, afraid of being found out, and as intolerant of others' stupidity as she was of her own. When she first came out of hiding in Cryck there had been a faint flutter of curiosity among the neighbourhood ladies, some of whom had seen her on television. She had been asked to a few sherry parties, turning up in appalling clothes, throwing her cigarette ends among the polished fire-irons, making no bones about her politics or her lack of interest in horses and in chasing wild animals. Cryck, she discovered with much relief, was out of social bounds. None of them would have anything to do with the Brigadier, a parvenu and impostor, or risk unpleasantness with the thugs who worked for him. There was no one else left in the place, except for the poor Chalmers. This was an excuse, if one were needed, not to ask any of them back. If they hadn't expected her to dress more suitably, clean her fingernails, get her hair cut, stop smoking, change her political views and show concern for the Royal Family, she might have done. Many of them were skilful gardeners and good gossips.

Their disapproval made her churlish. Anyway, she couldn't afford her own plonk, forget about the aperitifs and canapes.

Their dislike of Brigadier Wainwright, and the rumours she heard about his past, intrigued her at first. The Brig Boys of those days had long hair, ghoulishly unsuited to their great fists and shoulders, and were too doped and foolish to make much trouble. She had heard that Wainwright was piqued by her buying the place, but didn't take it seriously. Then, a few years ago, the younger lot started work, bullet-headed kids with sallow faces and ear-rings who had spent their childhoods in shacks and trailers; they were thin, jittery, angry; they came one hot June night and poured gallons of 2.4.5-T and diesel oil over her roses. A massacre.

She didn't remember that next morning very clearly, but she dreamed about it a lot. The dream and the reality might be confused – she didn't know. It was the first time she had seen Tyler House – a bizarre heap of gables and porticos, leaded lights and cupolas, hidden in dripping evergreen – and she had never seen it since. She made a loud noise in an uncarpeted, uncurtained room. There were a number of elderly men wearing tweed knickerbockers, golfing socks and narrow, polished brogues: perhaps a dozen, perhaps four, perhaps stuffed. There was a framed print of the Queen over the fireplace, a furled Union Jack, a packet of Bemax on the mantelpiece.

'I'll give you forty thousand for your roses, Mrs Broune,' one of the men said. 'I doubt whether you'll get a better offer.'

She woke up and went home; burned the roses and replaced them slowly, cheque by miserable cheque. The Brig Boys left her alone after that, but the people in the village were afraid to be seen talking to her and quickened their shuffle as they passed her gate.

The Sandersons had reminded Rebecca, for a while, of friends. They told her, before they left, that they felt guilty about selling to an elderly, genteel widow. 'Keep an eye on her?' they asked, without conviction. Though dreading her bouts of winter loneliness, Rebecca knew they wouldn't be as painful as the loneliness which used to attack her when she lived among people (that had been the killer, living indoors with people who never stopped talking). At times, in Cryck, she could forget herself. However craven and dispirited the village, limestone hills foamed with wild parsleys, goutweed, meadow-sweet, bearded hedges towered perilously over Roman lanes and bridlepaths, hellebores and orchids still grew in the woods and in summer the walls gave out a heat of their own, baking on the surface, last winter's chill slowly leaving the deep cavities. An immense sky, layer behind layer behind layer of sky always parting, dissolving, changing its course, arched dizzily from the horizons. Stare upwards, as Rebecca sometimes did, and you got vertigo, became unstable on the tilting earth.

This warm May evening, with *Rosa altaica* in flower and Primula smelling of Compline, all's well and time for a glass of Fine Fare Vino Bianco, Rebecca felt particularly secure. The little woman coming down the path – ('I thought you might be in the garden – I do hope you don't mind me barging in') – looked quite harmless. Rebecca hadn't spoken to anyone face to face for some weeks and this one, clean and pink and relatively unlined, looked anxious to please.

'I'm Mrs Muspratt – Phyllis Muspratt. I bought the Sandersons' cottage –'

'Of course. They told me.' Rebecca sucked a bleeding finger, wrung it in the air, grinned winsomely. 'Wish I could wear gloves.'

'Why can't you?' Phyllis asked, troubled.

The grin vanished. Rebecca picked up a bucket and set off up the path, a plume of smoke trailing behind her. 'You're not a gardener,' she stated, without turning round.

'I'm very keen on gardening,' Phyllis lied eagerly, 'but dreadfully ignorant, I'm afraid. My husband – my husband was the real gardener.'

Rebecca didn't feel this needed an answer. She dumped the bucket in an out-building halfway up the garden, plodded up the steps to the terrace, then suddenly thought of introducing herself: 'By the way, my name's Rebecca Broune. Pleased to meet you.' Again the frank grin, the hearty handshake. Someone must once have told her she was boyish, Phyllis thought, surprised by this flash of perspicacity.

'I know. The Sandersons told me. You're a writer, aren't you?' There was such a faint twitch of an eyebrow above the sunglasses, such a momentary chill, that she amended this to 'the writer' in the same breath.

'Well. Yes. I suppose so,' Rebecca said grudgingly. 'What about a glass of wine?'

'Oh – thank you – but really –'

'I'll get it. Take a seat.'

Phyllis chose the cane bucket chair, leaving the lounger to Mrs Broune. She felt proud of herself. There you are, it's quite easy to make friends, even with famous people, if you make the effort. Michael would have heard of Rebecca Broune, of course. Michael might even publish her. Just imagine if Michael published her and had to come and see her, to talk something over. She could cook supper for them both, sitting quietly doing her sewing while they had their discussion. Her cheeks flushed at the thought, her eyes sparkled.

Rebecca poured two tumblers of yellow wine and straddled the lounger. 'I hope the Brig Boys haven't been bothering you,' she said, looking up with one good eye over the flame of her lighter.

Phyllis was thinking she really must do something about the bathroom before she could ask anyone to supper. 'The who?'

'They're known round here as the Brig Boys. Rick Wainwright's gang, from the top of the hill ... The Brigadier,' she explained patiently.

'Oh, the Brigadier! So that's where they come from!' She couldn't contain herself any longer. 'My son's a publisher, you know.'

'Really. Did the Sandersons tell you why they left?'

'The Sandersons – oh no, they just said they needed something larger. I don't suppose it could possibly be the same –'

Rebecca sighed and jammed on her dark glasses. 'The same firm? I'm sure it couldn't. My publishers were Rowan and Jackson. Still are, I suppose.'

'No!' Phyllis bounced on her chair. She actually clapped her hands. 'I don't believe it! I simply don't believe it! Then you must know Michael! He's their chief editor now, but he's been there for years and years. Michael Muspratt?'

'I'm afraid not,' Rebecca snapped. 'I've had nothing to do with them for some time. Given it up, in fact.' God damn the woman, why can't she go back to Purley, wherever she came from? God damn the bloody little woman. She could see it all. The wretched man would visit his mother and come prying. She would be seen. Her silence would be vandalized. She would be handled, exposed, over the Soles Véronique. 'I suppose he'll be coming to see you,' she growled, sick to death behind her dark shields.

'Oh, of course! He's terribly busy but – I'll let you know, of *course*. Perhaps you could come round to supper or – .' What she could see of Mrs Broune's face below the sunglasses had set into granite folds. The cracked, fleshy lips were clamped together as if controlling pain. 'Are you all right?' Phyllis asked anxiously. 'Is something the matter?'

Rebecca was so angry, so distracted by loathing, that she threw her cigarette end into the mahonia. 'I'm not very sociable.'

'Of course. Well. Writers, I know, are ...' Phyllis gave up, not knowing what writers were. She had made a fool of herself, gushed too much. Nevertheless, the woman was extremely rude. Uncouth, really. She took a dainty portion of offence and visibly swallowed it. There was an uncomfortable silence. Birds hopped, foraging the newly mown grass; lilac hummed; the pale sky split above the valley, its fissures pouring eternal light. Dear Gerald, dear Surrey, children and summer years. Phyllis cleared her throat. 'You were saying something about the Brigadier ...'

'The Brig.' Rebecca revived. She took off her glasses, poured herself some more wine. 'He's not actually a Brigadier – not in any known army, anyway. He lives at Tyler's – Tyler House – up in the woods there. The Brig and his two brothers and his old Dad. He bought up the whole estate in the mid-sixties – everything except my place and yours, and Pip Chalmers' of course, though I hear he's got that now. That's why I asked if you'd had any trouble.'

Phyllis gave a little cough, turning her head as the smoke drifted towards her. 'What kind of trouble?'

'Oh, the sort of thing the Sandersons had. Upsetting their dustbins. Letting the cows loose. Setting fire to the hedge. Phone calls – you know, heavy breathing. Breaking windows, of course. Prowling about at night – that's quite a speciality. You mean you haven't heard them?'

'Only the motor bikes. And a radio sometimes. You don't mean the Brigadier – ?'

'Oh God, no. The Brig's too busy expanding his empire and planning his *coup*. No – the Brig Boys. They do all his dirty work. He brought in a whole gang twenty years ago, now it's mostly the sons. The original lot have gone on to better things – running the estate, making life hell for the tenants. You mean you haven't even seen the old man?'

Phyllis shook her head. It all sounded most unlikely, and yet ... 'What does *he* do?' she asked, with dread.

'He's stone-deaf and he walks. Even in mid-winter, walks for miles. Keeping an eye on things, I suppose. The story is that the Brig's the bastard son of a Lovejoy daughter – the Lovejoys owned the estate ever since sixteen-something – and that he bought it because she got rid of him. He was brought up by Barnardo's or something of the sort, ended by organizing fascist *coups* in very small countries round Indonesia. Nobody really knows. There's also a story that the old man was tracked down in a doss-house in Cardiff and brought to Tyler's before the Brig had ever met him. May be true, maybe not.' Rebecca's liveliness had been short-lived. What a waste of time this was. 'It all adds a certain something to life in Cryck. You'll get used to it.'

'I very much hope not!'

Rebecca saw a glimmer of hope. 'Well, Emma didn't, certainly. After Jack bought that bit of field she hardly dared go out. They let down her tyres, shat in the front garden – that sort of thing. And they make a lot of noise when roused. Shout

36

a lot. The kids got frightened. In the end they had to send them off to her mother's.'

'But why didn't they do something? Call the police?'

'Oh, the Brig's very friendly with the police. Well – perhaps "friendly" isn't the word. And there's no proof, after all – just that everyone knows, and the Brig Boys know that everyone knows, and that's the whole point. They'll get you out if they can – I promise you that.' Having her revenge on the little creature, Rebecca longed to be rid of her. 'It's hardly the right place, you know, for a peaceful retirement.'

'Oh dear.' Phyllis didn't know how much of this to believe. She remembered the bullies at school who had terrified the smaller girls with stories of men in the shrubbery, escaped lunatics, malevolent ghosts. She was still one of the smaller girls. 'I can't see why he should want my cottage – it's no use to a family, and there isn't much land –'

'Ah, but what there is belongs to the Brig by rights. We're the missing pieces of his jigsaw – maddening. Besides, who's to know your son isn't a Communist agent who's put you in there as a blind? Who's to know you're not a Communist agent, come to that.'

Phyllis giggled nervously. It was, of course, a joke. She mustn't give Mrs Broune the satisfaction of taking her seriously. 'But what about you? Your place is much bigger than mine and I'd have thought it was much more likely –'

'They're leaving me alone at the moment. Biding their time, I daresay.' The massacre of the roses was a private outrage, too near her murderous instincts for gossip. Anyway she'd done her best – with any luck young Muspratt would arrive just in time to move his mother out. She heaved herself up and came over with the wine bottle, but Phyllis put her hand over her glass.

'You live alone, I imagine.'

'Yes. It's quite a . . . change.' Rebecca recognized courage. It went with the cardigan. 'What about you? Are you – do you –?'

'Oh, I'm on my own, yes – divorced years ago. Not that one ever is, of course. They go on hanging round one's life in a maddening sort of way. Did you keep Slattery?'

'The gardener? I said I would, but he hasn't come. I've been meaning to contact him, but somehow ...'

'I shouldn't do that. They hate contact. Anyway he won't risk any trouble. You could always try offering him more money, of course – I imagine that's no problem?'

Really, she goes too far. Phyllis fastened the bottom button of her cardigan, put her feet side by side and prepared to leave. 'I was going to ask you if you could recommend a good builder,' she said, managing to imply that she now thought this most unlikely. 'A handyman is really what I need, but I know they're hard to come by.' She hadn't seen inside Rebecca's house, but could imagine it. 'The bathroom is quite disgusting and the whole place is very draughty. Also I need a lot more sockets. I don't know how people manage without plenty of sockets.'

Rebecca barked with laughter, though Phyllis couldn't see that she had said anything humorous. 'Your son's no good at that sort of thing? No. I suppose not. There are a couple of builders around, but they're both sharks. Unless ... I wonder ...' Rebecca took off her dark glasses and narrowed her good eye, sizing Phyllis up. She still seemed to be much amused. 'No. Perhaps not.'

'Perhaps not what?' Phyllis was beginning to have a headache and knew she sounded tart, but such theatricals irritated her.

'There's a fellow who works for the glass people over near Bamfield – Fred Skerry. He does odd jobs for ladies. But I don't think you'd get on.'

'I wasn't aware that one had to "get on" with one's handyman,' Phyllis said with dignity. 'Perhaps you would give me his telephone number.'

'Oh, you can't ring him up. You have to seek him out in Stores or somewhere. But I wouldn't advise it – you wouldn't get on at all.' Of course the little Muspratt didn't like her. Rebecca would have been surprised – not to say embarrassed – not to say intimidated – if she had. Still, she certainly had spirit. 'I'm quite handy with a screw-driver myself,' she mumbled. 'If I can be any help . . .'

'Perhaps you can advise me about the garden,' Phyllis said, gracious now. 'I sometimes feel quite helpless without Gerald.'

'Yes. You would. Well – any time. And if the Brig Boys annoy you, let me know. I'm always here.'

Phyllis walked briskly down the road. Rebecca had been another disappointment, but there you are – these things are sent to try us, and she wouldn't let herself be discouraged. What rubbish the woman talked. Communist agents, indeed. A herd of cows came wandering round the corner, bumping inertly, plodding up the hill sullen and submissive as old lags; a few were milling round her gate, watched idly by two louts in leather jackets and a mangy dog. She didn't care for cows and scrambled up the bank, laddering her good stockings no doubt, to let them pass. As they approached, she looked straight into the Brig Boys' featureless faces, the colour and texture of broken brick, and smiled her warmest, most fearless smile.

'Lovely evening,' she said. 'Do you think it'll last?'

The Brig Boys looked at each other. One said something to the other and they both burst out laughing, hitting each other on the back, hitting their own thighs, hitting the cows, hitting each other again. They rolled and rollicked up the hill, still laughing, and the cows shat themselves and the Brig Boys' boots skidded and slithered and one of them fell in a pile of muck and they laughed so much that the dog stood still, patiently waiting with one raised paw until they came to their senses.

5

Sophia knew that Bron was having an affair – 'a thing' she would have called it, if she had spoken or even thought about it – though she didn't know with whom. It was something you had to live with, like carbon monoxide and nuclear war – a threat of extinction lurking in every moment of the day and too fearful to contemplate. He, poor love, brought it to her attention by snapping unnecessarily at the children, bringing home extravagant presents, going on a diet, offering to do things like moving Mother to Cryck. She wished he could be more secretive, though realized that such consideration was hard in marriage.

Bron believed he was being secretive. He was worn out with the effort of deceiving her. He didn't do this for Sophia's sake – he couldn't believe he was all that important to her – but for his own. He loved Sophia. He needed her. He loved his children. His domestic life was extremely satisfactory on the whole. He refused to believe that a natural urge might be putting all this in jeopardy. He was managing it, he thought, with the utmost discretion, and God knows it was hard work.

Sophia appreciated his efforts and did her best to co-operate with them. She understood, far better than he did, why it was necessary for him to be sexually unfaithful to her. This didn't alter the fact that if it were brought out into the open, dragging with it all its implications and complications, she would be devastated. Rightly or wrongly, that would be it. She could only survive this by putting one foot in front of the other, groping for familiar landmarks and keeping her eyes tight shut. When she opened them, the danger might have receded, though she knew it would never go entirely away. Amiable and good-looking, Bron would always need something on the side to keep himself upright.

Sophia was aware of this, but there was a great deal more

she didn't know, and would have scoffed at if she had been told. That she was a great deal more intelligent than Bron, for instance; that her talent for design, now used only to amuse children, was potentially more valuable than his, which was unlikely to get him further than a drawing board in an advertising agency; that her personality, which she thought of as timid, was remarkably powerful and difficult to compete with. Nor did she know how beautiful she was, lumbering along with the pushchair and the shopping bag, dressed like an old man in shapeless trousers and threadbare overcoat. 'Total rubbish!' she would have said; or, in one of her more light-hearted moods, 'Fiddlesticks!' When she expostulated like this, Phyllis came into her face for an instant before it was clouded again by more adult cares and responsibilities.

These unacknowledged facts, far more than Bron's minor attachments, made for tension in the family. Sophia and Bron thought of it as inevitable wear and tear, and had learned to withdraw from each other when it threatened to become painful. Bron, whose disposition was more open than Sophia's, had tried to have it out with her in the early years – 'What's troubling you?', 'Nothing. I'm fine', 'Come on, love – out with it!', 'Nothing. Really. I'm fine. Just a bit tired, that's all.' He had never got further than that. There was nothing to be done about it. He had the odd affair, without rancour, and watched a lot of television or read old copies of *What Car* until it had blown over. Sophia, getting through it, went to bed at nine, cooked unnecessarily for the freezer, washed the cushion covers. When they met again after a few days, they were glad to see each other and perfectly friendly, neither of them referring to the bits of suspicion and guilt that might be littered about.

At the moment, a May weekend, they were in a state of withdrawal. Bron had, he said, gone to the office to finish a lay-out; he couldn't work at home with the kids around. Sophia, who knew that he had not gone to the office, told Jasper, aged six, that he had. Jasper, unknown to his mother, telephoned the office to tell his father that he had seen two Black Redstarts in the park. There was no reply. Sophia told Jasper that Bron's extension was switched off at weekends. Jasper, correctly sensing a pack of lies, locked himself in the lavatory and refused to come out. As he had deliberately left the safety gate open, Selina crawled up the stairs and fell down them again. She screamed for half an hour, more at the insult than the injury. Sophia yelled at Jasper through the locked door. She kicked the cat and shouted at Selina to *shut up* even while she was hugging her and feeling for broken bones. Although no one but mother and child was making any noise, the effect was pandemonium. When the telephone started to ring Jasper, who had been peacefully turning the pages of last week's Colour Supplement, threw it down and covered his ears. Godammit, he muttered, *godammit*.

Sophia took a deep breath. She reached to the top shelf of the dresser, took two chocolate buttons out of the bag without looking and plugged Selina's mouth in full scream. Carrying the child on her hip, she walked very slowly to the telephone, picked up the receiver, paused, then gave her number in a voice so controlled that it sounded, to the caller, sepulchral.

'Darling,' her mother said, 'are you all right? Were you in the middle of something?'

'Only life,' Sophia said. She suddenly felt near tears. At times like this she almost wished she smoked or took heroin. She sat down at the kitchen table, lowering Selina with care, as though the child were an injured part of herself. 'How's everything going?'

'Very well. I was wondering about the whooping cough.'

'That seems to be all right. I mean they haven't got it, as far as I know.'

'My dear child, you'd certainly know if they had. You didn't have them inoculated, did you?'

'Of course not.' Patiently, Sophia picked the conversation up again and pointed it away from her. 'What have you been doing? How's the weather?'

'Oh, I've been very busy. I went to call on Rebecca Broune.'

'Who?'

'Rebecca Broune. The writer. She lives just up the road.'

'My God, Mother, you are going it. I thought she was dead. Did you have intellectual conversation?'

'Not at all. She's a very keen gardener. To tell you the truth,' – Phyllis lowered her voice, but who could be listening? – 'I didn't care for her very much. She's not an easy woman.'

'Oh dear. I'm sorry.' Sophia extricated her hair from Selina's clutches and put her on the floor. The child pondered a moment, then crawled like an energetic crab towards a plate of cat food. 'I'm sorry, Mother. Hang on just a minute ... Sorry. So have you met anyone else? Hasn't there been a delegation from the Women's Institute or the Friends of Rural England or whatever they have down there?'

'Not yet, I'm expecting them at any moment. I was thinking, darling –'

'And what about the gardener? What's his name? Has he showed up yet?'

'Not yet. I'm going to search him out tomorrow. I suppose Jasper's back at school?'

'It's a State school, Mother. He's been back for weeks. It's nearly half-term. Lina, *stop it*! ... Sorry about that.'

'What was she doing?'

'Turning on the gas.'

'You mean she can stand up now? I didn't know she was standing.'

'She can pull herself up. Lina! *No*! Hang on, Mother ...' She picked Selina up, went out into the hall and shouted up the stairs. 'Jasper! I want you to look after Lina for a bit! Will you come down *now*!'

Phyllis, waiting, heard no more after this but a distant thudding, then silence. Just as she was going to ring off, Sophia's voice began approaching down the telephone line. 'It's your own fault! ... I've *told* you never to lock the loo door ... For God's sake get in there and do what you're told for once! ... *Jesus*! ...' Then, breathless, 'Sorry, Mother. He'd locked himself in.'

'Jasper? In where?'

'The upstairs loo. I don't know how many times I've asked Bron to take the lock off. Anyway. Where were we? Have you spoken to Michael?'

'Not lately, no. When is Jasper's –'

'Don't you think it's time he showed some signs of getting married?'

'Who? Jasper?'

'*No*, Mother. Michael. It's not as though he's gay or anything. Can't you find him some nice girl down there? You know. Wholesome?'

'I very much doubt it ... Are you all right, Sophia?'

'Yes. Of course I am. Why? Don't I sound it?'

'Well ... You sound harassed. But then, you always do. I wish you could send Jasper –'

'When is he going to see you? Have you asked him?'

'Michael? Oh, I don't know. Yes, of course I've asked him. He's very busy, you know.'

'He's got no *ties*. He's just lazy, that's all. He should certainly go and see you.'

'Well. I think so too. But there you are. Couldn't you come down at half-term –'

'Hang on a minute, Mother ... There's a ghastly silence. I'd better go and see what they're doing.'

'Or maybe Bron could bring Jasper and leave him with me – then you could have the weekend on your own, I mean just with Selina –'

'We'll think about it. I haven't the faintest idea when half-term is. I really must go, Mother.' Separated from Selina for five minutes, chasms of fear threatened. 'Oh my God, all hell's broken loose in there. Sorry – take care – I'll ring you –'

*

Rebecca Broune was, at the same time, talking to her daughter

Isabel, who had telephoned from a public callbox in Mottsley Hospital, transferring the charge. She had been taken there six months ago, after an unsuccessful suicide attempt. Rebecca hadn't spoken to her since then and felt the call was ominous. She wouldn't have answered the phone if she hadn't happened to be indoors at that moment. One of the reasons she wished she were a man was the ease with which they could pee, simply unzipping where they stood, not thinking about it. No wonder women were handicapped; the time they had to spend relieving themselves must add up to years of valuable life. Carrying the receiver on a long lead, she poured herself a glass of wine as she talked, searched for her lighter, tucked in her shirt and fastened her jeans with some effort, lit a cigarette.

'Well, Isabel. How are you? What's the problem?'

Knowing all too well that the problem was a mistaken weekend in Penzance thirty-six years ago. The sins of the fathers might visit – though she couldn't even remember what he looked like, except for a rather large mole on his left shoulder-blade – but it was the sins of the mothers that went on and on, never to be forgiven or forgotten.

'I just felt like talking to you.'

Some misguided psychiatrist, no doubt. A wise look, a casual suggestion – don't you think you should contact your mother? Irresponsible lot. 'Any particular reason?' she asked, as though there couldn't be.

'Not really.' A whimper – it might be laughter. 'Sunday evening, I expect. Everyone's gone home.'

'Everyone?'

'Well. Most of them. I felt a bit bored.'

That would serve. The last thing she wanted to do was pry. 'How are you getting on, anyway?'

'Oh, better. I'm much better. They're talking of letting me. They're talking of letting me out soon.'

'Good. That's good.' With reluctance, with dread, Rebecca made herself ask the obvious question. 'What are your plans?'

'Well ... I don't know. I suppose I'll take a room some-where.'

Although she couldn't see Isabel – small, thin, vaguely rat-like? – Rebecca could see the room clearly. It had a gas meter, a skylight, some sort of runner over the formica-topped table. The handle was loose on the door, layers of brown paint on the finger-plate. It smelt of old tea and leaking gas. 'And do what?' she asked cheerfully.

'Get a job. I don't know ...' The girl – of course she was no longer a girl – sounded as though during the course of this conversation she had gone through some debilitating ordeal. Rebecca pushed her fingers through her hair so that it stood up on end. I will not be blamed. I will not be held responsible. 'That sounds very sensible,' she said.

'Yes ... Well ... The only thing is ...'

'Yes? ... Isabel? ... Are you still there?'

But they seemed to have been cut off. Not knowing the number of the callbox, Rebecca told herself that she couldn't ring back. There were ways of fiddling with those gas meters. 'Damn!' she swore loudly. 'Damn, damn, damn!' then hurried out to her roses, where she could feel the soothing influence of love.

*

Michael knew he should telephone his mother. He actually began to dial before he realized that he was phoning home; not only that, but he was expecting his father to answer. He didn't know the Cryck number off-hand, and his address book was on the other side of the room. There was a concert on Radio 3 in ten minutes. He stayed where he was in the armchair, looking round at Sunday evening: late sunlight through the tall sash windows, newspapers, cushions, glossy dust-covers, records, plants, good furniture. It was pleasant. It was acceptable. It was empty. He was used to it.

Michael doubted his own reality. He thought about this a great deal. It puzzled him. Obviously he existed – people

46

spoke to him, reacted to him, touched his body. In calling him by his name – Muspratt, Mike, Mickey, Michael – they clearly recognized him, even at a distance. Why, then, didn't he recognize himself? Half the time he even forgot what he looked like, stepping to one side to avoid his image in shop windows and glass doors, vaguely troubled by the familiarity of an overcoat or a tie. Everything he did, he felt, was chicanery. He continually expected to be found out.

Not only expected it, but looked forward to it. That was the main problem. Nothing as simple as an identity crisis, all that tedious dither in women's novels. The last thing he wanted was to 'find himself'. What he wanted was to be erased. Removed from the files. To be – if that was possible, since the important thing was never to have been at all – an illusion.

It had seemed imperative to keep this from his father, who did not accommodate illusions. Without ever saying so, Gerald had expected a great deal of his only son and placidly gone on expecting it, even after Sophia had shown herself to be much more capable. Michael had learned very early in his life – it had been an instinctive, unconscious process at first – that the easiest and most gratifying way of satisfying Gerald was to impersonate him. By the time Michael left Cambridge their voices, their mannerisms and personal habits, had become almost identical. This was as far as it went, but it had kept Gerald happy and given Michael a serviceable image. The old man's death, so uncharacteristically sudden and rash, had not only been Michael's greatest tragedy but had left him gasping and floundering, his nonentity ripped untimely from his father's tomb, put on its nonexistent feet and expected to carry on. After two and a half years he still felt like a shadow deserted by its subject, painfully conscious of his lack of self, half-hearted. He had been told that he was shy: it served.

Not surprising, then, that at the age of forty-four he was still unmarried. Anyway, it didn't surprise him; he never even contemplated it. Except once, with troubled Mary, but she had gone off to Zimbabwe and stopped writing. He could no longer remember what had seemed special about Mary, except that she was plain. And vulnerable. Yes, she had winced a lot, though not in bed. Apart from that, his memories of her were as vague as his ideas of what life would have been like if he had married her. Much like other people's, he supposed; different.

He had a number of friends, most of them dating back to his Cambridge days, a few from his minor but reputable school. Some of them had already replaced their original wives or husbands; some had teenage children; one Newnham girl, now a high-powered executive in Revlon or Lancôme, something like that, was a grandmother. They were all fond of Michael. He served so many purposes – escort, confidant, uncle, best man, godfather, emergency bank, adviser, jobbing gardener, chauffeur, reference library, booking agency, Santa Claus, good friend – everything, in fact, except lover. Against their own interests, they sometimes tried to pair him off with a new acquaintance. 'She seems a very nice girl – works in television/the B.B.C./journalism/Sotheby's/the Zoo. We've told her what a crusty old bachelor you are. Now do make an effort, love.'

And sometimes he did, and occasionally it worked and they wouldn't see him for a few weeks; but sooner or later, to their relief, he came shambling back, shy as ever with his bank manager's air of neutral goodwill, his old-fashioned tweeds, mocking them with small secrets. Then the women kissed him and the men felt like it but punched him instead, and the teenage children were reassured that everything was as bloody boring as it ought to be and the animals purred or wagged, according to their species. The new acquaintance was always dropped, and the friends gradually became less eager in their match-making. They preferred to keep him to themselves.

Michael was grateful to them. Without them – certainly since his father's death – he would have dissolved entirely. He didn't feel about them as they felt about him; if he did, he would be one of them, and the situation would be different. No, he was used to them; they had literally grown on him, like his beard and the hair on his chest and the ageing skin under his Adam's apple. In their terms, he was probably very attached to them; in his own, attachment was a mingling of shadows.

Which brought him back to his mother, a woman who silently implored him to tackle Probate, deal with the Department of Social Security, inspect drains, approve contracts and agreements; a woman who expected him to look after her. She had never said so. All right – but that was what his father had done, and how could she distinguish between them? She was surprisingly astute, often disconcerted him by her silences, but even so she obviously had no idea of his true incompetence. Look how she had behaved over the funeral, piling responsibility on responsibility – 'You must ask my son about that ... My son would like ... My son feels ...' He had managed it all, by some miracle, but it had stretched his capacities to breaking point. Then that appalling remark when, behaving as adequately as he could, he had taken her out to lunch: 'That wasn't Gerald. You mustn't think of that as Gerald' – as though he, the old man's alter-ego, his spitting image, chipped from that block, his *son* for Christ's sake, had never known him at all. (Well, he didn't know you. That's different.) It was typical of women – he knew his anger made him unreasonable – that a mere sexual connection should give them such status, such arrogance. Patronizing bitch. Though he knew how she mourned. So what was he supposed to do about it?

He was so enraged and shocked by his thoughts that he forgot the concert.

'Mother?'

'Michael! I *am* glad. How are you, darling?'

'I'm fine. And you?'

'Very well indeed. It's so lovely here. You'll never guess who lives down the road – Rebecca Broune!'

'Good God. Yes, of course – she does live somewhere out there –'

'In Cryck, actually.'

'Cryck. Yes, that's right. We used to publish her, you know.'

'Yes, dear. She told me. So what are you doing with yourself? Getting out of London much?'

'No – no, not at all, actually. Terribly busy just now – spring lists and so on. Have you got any help?'

'Help?'

'Well, you know – the house and so on. Help with the garden.'

'I expect the gardener will come soon, and Mrs Broune told me of a handyman. So I'm well set up. You mustn't worry.'

'I'm not worrying.'

'Good. That's good, then.'

'Are you thinking of coming up to London at all?'

'I certainly wasn't thinking of it. Why, darling?'

'Well. If you were, we could have lunch.'

'Yes. But, you see, I'm not.'

'No. Well, if you do.'

'Of course. Are you all right, Michael?'

'Yes, I'm fine. I'll come and see you some time, when I can get away.'

'That would be lovely. Any time. I really look forward to it.'

'Yes. Well. Sorry I couldn't help with the move, but it was really impossible –'

'Of course. Bron was splendid. You just come when you can.'

'Yes, I will. Well ... just wanted to check up on you. I've got to rush, so talk to you soon. Good-bye, Mother.'

'Good-bye, darling. Thank you for ringing. Good-bye ...'

*

The miles unfurled at a click: sunshine in Cryck, rain over the Cotswolds, drizzle in Oxford, mist on the Chilterns, scattered cloud over Beaconsfield, evening far gone in Ealing, twilight in Hampstead and Willesden Green. Lorries took four hours to cover that distance; impatient lovers, people speeding to deathbeds, couldn't do it in less than two; even passengers in jet planes had time to age between the Mendips and Heathrow. Phyllis, Sophia, Michael, Isabel and Rebecca Broune were returned to their own lives at approximately twice the speed of light. Whatever had happened between them seemed insubstantial, but could change their history.

Phyllis was determined not to be intimidated by Rebecca's stories about the Brigadier. She was sure they were grossly exaggerated. The Brig Boys certainly made her very nervous – she had never encountered that sort of person before, two years' National Service was what they needed – but that was all the more reason for making it perfectly clear that she was here to stay. She was no longer waiting for Gerald to take over and she wasn't going to be put off by foolish rumours.

She had decided to contact Slattery immediately Rebecca had warned her not to. The postman told her that Slattery lived in the cottage on the corner, thatched, a bit of a front garden, she couldn't miss it. He then called in on Slattery and told him to expect her, so Slattery put on his jacket and sat by the range, looking ill, while his wife stuffed things under cushions and put the kettle on. Not that she was going to offer Mrs Muspratt a cup of tea, but it looked better to have a steaming kettle.

'You won't go working for her,' she stated.

Slattery shook his head. 'Not worth it,' he said.

Slattery had been born in Rebecca Broune's cottage and remembered Cryck before the Brigadier came. In those days women used to gather and gossip outside, summer evenings; the village still belonged to the Lovejoys, the banks were mown, there was a parson in the Rectory. Bill had moved away when he was a lad, and when he came back in '68 to work for the Chalmers the Brigadier had bought up just about everything. Major Chalmers tried to buy a cottage for him but the Brig wouldn't sell, so the Major rented it on a lease and looked after it. When the Major died, Mrs Pip took over, no trouble; but the very day she died, the Brig sent a note round to remind them the lease was up in August. He couldn't actually turn them out, Slattery knew that, but they might as well give up if he wanted to. Slattery had retired now, he and Ellen managing on their pensions, all they had bar the thousand pounds Mrs P. had left in her Will, but they wouldn't see that before winter. The whole village knew that the Brig was mad as hell not to have got the Sandersons' place – Mrs Muspratt's stay would be short and nasty, no question of that.

Still, he wasn't going to turn her down flat. He'd hear what she had to offer. You never knew when the Brig might pop off, and the rest of them wouldn't be up to much without him. Slattery was a frightened old man, but he was cunning. Ellen didn't trust him to take care of his own interests. She stood close to him, arms folded across her apron, trying to stop him from getting a word in edgeways.

'I think you went to the Sandersons on Saturdays?' Phyllis said, beaming at them from the edge of her seat. 'So I was hoping –'

'That was when he was working at Mrs Chalmers,' Ellen said. 'That was the only day, then, bar Sundays, and of course he don't work Sundays. He's retired now. We've got the pension to consider.'

'Well, of course. Any other day would do just as well.'

'He's a good little worker,' Ellen said, 'but he can't do nothing heavy, it's his back, he's had a back for ever so long.'

'Me back's all right,' Slattery mumbled, shrunken in his chair, eyes flicking from woman to woman. He wasn't going to work for her, but he wasn't going to have himself downpriced either.

'Mr Sanderson did all the heavy up there. Bill just did the borders and such. Didn't you, Bill?'

Slattery ignored her. 'What will you be doin' with that bit of field?' he asked, fixing Phyllis with a rheumy eye.

'I don't know.' Such a bright little person, she felt, altogether too eager. 'What do you think?'

'It's no good. Full of squidge. Not much you can do with that.'

'They should never have bought that bit of field,' Ellen said, swelling her chest and pursing her lips. 'That wasn't necessary.'

'I don't want no trouble,' Slattery said, as though that settled something.

Phyllis felt out of her depth. Gerald would have known how to deal with this man; he would have respected Gerald. She went back to the beginning and started again: 'I think Mr Sanderson paid you £1.50 an hour?'

They nodded, thinking of other things.

'So I was wondering whether two pounds ...'

They said nothing. The kettle steamed. The clock ticked. Mrs Slattery looked out of the window, as though preparing to remark on the weather.

'£2.25, perhaps,' Phyllis said desperately. It was much more than she had paid Mr Rodburn, but she really needed someone to bring in the coal and chop logs – the borders were the least of it.

They still said nothing, but Mrs Slattery stopped looking out of the window.

'I live alone,' Phyllis ventured. 'So I really do need you, you see. Mr Sanderson seemed to think it was quite certain –'

That was hopeless. Slattery's toothless mouth sagged with contempt.

'Well,' she snapped. 'Will you come or not?'

They didn't answer. She might as well take it for an acceptance.

'Which day, then? Monday?'

'Betty comes over Mondays, don't she, Bill. You wouldn't want to go out Mondays.'

'Any day, then. Wednesday?'

Mrs Slattery couldn't seem to think of anything against Wednesday. She glared at her husband.

'Depends,' Slattery said.

'Well, I *would* like to know.' Phyllis laughed, admitting this was ridiculous. 'Shall we say Wednesday?'

'You never know what might come up,' Slattery said.

Phyllis knew the interview was at an end. It was the best she could do. They made no attempt to see her out, so the little speech she had prepared about Slattery's marigolds and candytuft and love-in-the-mist, all neatly bordered by shells and pebbles, was wasted. A huge horse-chestnut bearing a thousand candles hung over Slattery's wall and a great Gean cherry had snowed all over his bank. He must have some human quality somewhere; he couldn't be all bones and greed and swindle.

The only question Slattery had asked her was what she was going to do with her bit of field. She ought to have given him a definite answer – vegetable garden, tennis court, swimming pool? – instead of asking him what he thought. Full of squidge, whatever that was. She knotted her cardigan round her shoulders and set off down to the stream, sitting herself on a tree-stump with her chin in her hand and trying to visualize the transformation of this unpromising, unhappy patch. The sun was low over the opposite hills, the cool shadows long on the side of the house and under the trees. Cows had already blundered against the chicken wire fence and would soon knock it down altogether. She ought to call on the Brigadier and discuss it with him. Perhaps when Michael came ... Her thoughts drifted off towards Michael, Sophia, Jasper, her familiars.

She was almost asleep when a cloud passed over the sun and she felt a sudden chill in the air. She shivered, and half-turned to unknot the cardigan. The old man was standing immediately behind her, so close that she could smell his heavy breath and see the veins in his eyes. He might have been there for half an hour, for ever.

'Oh!' she screamed, though with no more noise than a rabbit, scrambling to her feet, facing him across the wire, her heart pounding. 'Oh! I didn't – I wasn't –'

The old man stared. Propped up against the sky, he was enormous. His nose spread like a fungus; the lobes of his ears were pendulous and purple; he had the hauteur of the totally deaf.

'You must be – Mr Wainwright?' Foolishly, she held out her hand over the makeshift fence, then dropped it, then indicated the surrounding land as though miming a nursery song. 'This is your son's field.'

He didn't move, the breathing loud and steady.

'I was just wondering about the fence. I was going to come and see the Brigadier. I thought perhaps we could come to – some arrangement?'

Not a flicker. He breathed and stared, stared and breathed.

'It's not that I mind,' she said. 'It's the cows. Perhaps they'd be ... safer?'

He said something. She didn't catch what it was, or wasn't sure she had heard him correctly. 'I'm sorry?' she asked, almost leaning towards him, impatiently pushing the hair out of her eyes as though it hindered her hearing.

He didn't repeat it. He turned and walked away across the field, very slow, measured, up and down the dips, in and out of shadow until, between one moment and the next, he disappeared.

Phyllis stayed at home all Wednesday and Thursday waiting for Slattery, but he didn't come. By Friday morning she was angry. This did her more good than all her efforts to be reasonable. If the Brigadier was fool enough to think he could get rid of her by blackmailing Slattery and sending his dreadful old father to spy on her (and frighten her out of her wits) – too absurd, but that's what it looked like – then Phyllis Muspratt, a soldier's daughter, would go to war.

The first thing was to put up a solid, permanent boundary – a wall would be best, but it would take too long. It seemed to her that she had plenty of money – the Surrey house had fetched three times as much as the cost of the cottage, and any sums over three figures had always been dealt with by Gerald. She had noticed a fencing company on the way into Lamberts Heath and drove there very fast, keeping a stony profile as she sped past Slattery's cottage.

A girl with a streaming cold – she shouldn't be out really – pushed a dog-eared pamphlet across the desk and went back to blowing her nose.

'I don't think I want timber lap,' Phyllis said, rejecting the picture of a young woman in a bikini sitting doing absolutely nothing in a small compound. 'It's a field, you see.'

'Well, that's all we do.'

'But it says on your board that you do all types of fencing –'

'That's right.'

'And I don't want timber lap.'

The girl shrugged, trying to find a dry corner of her handkerchief.

Finally the local branch of a London estate agent, hushed and superior, sent her to Ringwood Estates twenty miles away. When she got there the office was closed for lunch. She drove to the nearest town and bought an electric hedge-trimmer; the picture on the instructions showed a young woman in peep-toe sandals trimming privet. By the time she got back to the office there was a Range Rover parked outside and a ginger, cavalry-twill young man sitting at a desk. His name was Mr Weaver, he'd only been in this job a couple of weeks, came from Hampshire actually. They were happy together, inspecting half-round rails and sawn timber, pale and weave, field and orchard and portcullis gates. He would come and look at the site tomorrow morning, no sense in hanging about, Mr Weaver knew just what she wanted.

He arrived punctually next day, wearing a hacking jacket and a checked cap. She wondered whether he might not think her bit of the field rather small, since he was clearly used to dealing with parks and forests, but he was extremely polite and measured it and said they could put up sturdy post-and-rail round that in a couple of days, no problem at all. He thought she should definitely have a gate for access, Keruing Hardwood preferably, an Estate would look best but a ten-by-four Diamond Braced would be perfectly adequate. He wrote it all down with a gold pencil in a large notebook and accepted a glass of sherry after glancing at his digital watch.

Mr Weaver was as good as his word. A great pile of posts and rails was delivered on Wednesday; two clean young men, a very different breed from the Brig Boys, arrived on Thursday. They took down the old fence, rolling it into bales, and fixed transistorized electric wire round the boundary to stop the Brigadier's wandering cows. A couple of myopic heifers bumped it with their muzzles and stepped delicately back; by mid-afternoon the whole herd was gathered round the Muspratt field, enjoying a welcome distraction. They were joined by a muttering group of Brig Boys, who obviously didn't know what to make of it. Phyllis was glad to see that Mr Weaver's young men didn't fraternize, but got on with their work; she was relieved, nevertheless, when the Brig Boys left. Without the chicken wire she felt horribly exposed.

When she drew back her curtains next morning, the young

58

men's truck was already parked in the lane. She went downstairs, put the kettle on, unlocked the back door and went out to see if they'd like a cup of tea. They were running about the field, shouting. The garden was full of cows – they must have been there for some time, because there were cow-pats everywhere and the borders were trampled. Now, in dull bovine panic, they were blundering about while the young men shouted and waved their arms. Not only that, but the posts that had been set in yesterday had been chopped down, the metal stakes which held the electric wire had been uprooted and thrown about the field, the connecting wire torn out of the transistor, the batteries gone. The young man who told her all this – she could hardly understand a word – hurried indoors to phone Mr Weaver; the other, arming himself with a broom handle, whacked cows through the front gate into the lane, where they milled about, not knowing whether to go up or down. Phyllis helped him, in her dressing gown, bold with rage.

Mr Weaver arrived within the hour, bringing new batteries and a portly, uncommunicative colleague in a business suit, whom he introduced as our Mr Bright. Thankful to see them, Phyllis poured out all she knew of the Brigadier and his Boys, what Mrs Broune had told her they'd done to the Sandersons, everything up to her encounter with the old man the other evening. Mr Weaver looked curiously sheepish; he kept glancing quickly at Mr Bright, who was even more curiously impassive. They went out to inspect the damage. Mr Bright came back and asked for the Deed of Sale and relevant plans. Phyllis gave them to him and he returned to the field to confer with Mr Weaver, holding the plans taut against the breeze that flattened his trouser legs and lifted his few spikes of hair. Mr Weaver came back and asked Phyllis if she would mind coming out for a moment. Phyllis had expected him to be angry but he was melancholy and formal, as though at an expected death.

'Who erected the original fence?' Mr Bright asked.

'I don't know. The Sandersons, I imagine. They bought the land first.'

'Then it's more likely, I think, to have been –' Mr Bright struggled with the papers, hitting them smartly with the back of his hand, 'Mrs Chalmers?'

'Perhaps it was, but she's dead now and anyway –'

'Just a moment, dear lady. Whoever it was, we must assume the boundary was correct at the time. There were no disputes, as far as you know.'

'That doesn't –'

'Look here, if you will.' He squatted clumsily and poked a stick into a small hole in the ground. 'This was the position of the wire fence, I take it.'

Mr Weaver nodded miserably.

'I'm afraid the new posts were fixed outside that line, not inside it. You understand?'

'No,' Phyllis said.

'Six inches,' Mr Bright said, helping himself up. 'By some unfortunate oversight, you have taken six inches of Brigadier Wainwright's land.'

She would have laughed if Mr Weaver hadn't looked so tragic. 'But he's got thousands of acres! Anyway, why didn't he just come and tell me? It'd have been cheaper to buy six inches of his wretched land!'

'It's the principle,' Mr Bright said. 'If you will allow me, you seem to have been grossly misinformed, madam. Brigadier Wainwright is a very – shall we say "influential" figure in our part of the world. "Greatly to find quarrel in a straw" – or in this case post – "when honour's at the stake" – eh, Weaver?'

He glared at Mr Weaver, who smiled like a wince of pain; he would have supported himself on his shooting stick, if he had thought to bring it with him. 'I'm afraid it's entirely my responsibility,' he mumbled. 'I should have looked at the plans, instead of assuming –'

'But that's not the *point*!' Phyllis burst out. 'What about destroying my property? What about yours – the wire and the batteries and everything? It's an outrage!'

'I suggest you place the posts nine inches within the boundary line,' Mr Bright said. 'A foot would be even better. Now if you don't mind, Weaver, I should be on my way.' He folded the plans neatly and handed them back to her. 'I'm afraid that moral issues are not within my province, Mrs ... Delighted to have met you. Good day.'

'But I'm not going to let them get away with it!' Phyllis protested to Weaver as they followed Mr Bright up the hill. 'The Brigadier must pay for the posts and your electric thing – I shall sue him if necessary!'

Mr Weaver stopped so suddenly that she nearly fell over him. 'My dear Mrs Muspratt, I do beg of you to do no such thing. It would only make matters worse – much worse. The mistake was entirely mine. I will bring the new posts over in the morning myself. Do, I entreat you, ignore this little incident!'

He was so passionate, so earnest, that Phyllis was touched. She almost patted his ginger whiskers. 'You mean ... pretend I didn't notice?' she asked incredulously. 'Even the cows?'

'Exactly. I'll tell the lads to fix up the wire well within the boundary line and I'll come myself, over the weekend, to get the fence up for you.' His pale blue eyes pleaded with her – nothing could be fairer than that?

Michael in grey shorts, socks round his ankles, a cricket ball through the greenhouse roof ... 'All right, Mr Weaver,' she said reluctantly. 'But next time, I promise you ...'

'Jolly good!' he said, and bounded after Mr Bright. She watched them leave, puzzled. Surely it was wrong of them to give in so easily? And yet – what a nice young man. How good of him to take the blame.

*

Mr Weaver brought the new posts in his Range Rover, though it meant two journeys; and he did, indeed, work by himself all Saturday afternoon and the whole of Sunday. How had he been supposed to know that Wainwright owned a controlling interest in Ringwood Estates? He had not only nearly lost his job, he was paying for the ruined posts out of his own pocket. He worked in a frenzy, hauling the twelve-foot rails down the hill, sawing and hammering, his freckled back vulnerable (Phyllis guessed) to the hot sun. He hammered the posts in a foot or so and sawed off the tops, not liking to do a shoddy job, but according to Bright they wouldn't be there long anyway and the old bird wouldn't know the difference.

Phyllis thought he would stop for a plate of cold beef and salad or at least a glass of beer, but no, he was possessed. By Sunday afternoon, when she took him a cup of tea, there was something new in his expression, a kind of ferret look he didn't have before. 'Damned silly, if you ask me,' he said, 'to chop up a perfectly good field.' She was just going back to the house when he added, 'Since you're here, you can give me a hand with the gate,' without so much as please, as though he didn't know she was an elderly woman.

The gate was very heavy. Mr Weaver did take most of the weight, but even so it was a struggle to keep her end up while he heaved it on to wooden blocks; then the blocks weren't high enough and he sent her to get two more from the Range Rover – yes, sent her – and it was more push and heave until at last he got the heel on to the hanging post and dismissed her with a curt nod, not of thanks, but as much as to say she could get on with something else.

It was almost dark by the time he finished. She insisted on giving him a whisky and soda but he drank it in a hurry, not like a tired man at the end of the day. Then he said the bill would be posted, shook her hand in a distracted way and left, running down the front path.

Later on she took a torch and went out, finding the moon so bright that a torch was unnecessary. She walked down the field and leant on her gate. The new fence cast a shadow. She could hear animals – cows, she hoped – swishing and shuffling. She thought she heard footsteps, a kind of creaking on the grass, but when she shone the torch there was nothing. Perhaps it had been a rabbit or a badger. Perhaps a fox slinking by. There were a lot of strange noises if you listened carefully: calls from trees, wings, short howls as though some creature had been suddenly strangled, the itching of grass disturbed by insects and worms. She stayed there, growing chilly and against her will, to prove her indifference to anyone who might be watching from the dense shadow of the stream.

Isabel's phone call troubled Rebecca like an old wound. She tried not to pay attention to it, as she tried not to attend to the other aches and discomforts of her spirit, but it was so troublesome that even in June, when she should have been completely absorbed, she was distracted. It was impossible to conjure love out of thin air – the air surrounding Rebecca and her children was rarefied to the point of being unbreathable – but money might serve. How to get money? As she moved with untypical gentleness and care between Reine des Violettes and Empress Josephine, inspecting their buds and leaves and stems for any imperfection, and paused by *Rosa* 'Pomponia', hoping to catch a trace of its fragrance through the smoke that clung to her always, and reached up to Madame Staechelin, raising the head of one bloom with a finger, as she might have raised the head of a shy child if she had been that sort of woman, Rebecca tried to think what she could sell, pawn, mortgage. Since the answer was always the same she finally, with an exasperated sigh, went indoors and telephoned Ralph.

'I have to come to London this week – can we have a talk?'

The deep, imperturbable cantor's voice: 'I have to go to Tokyo on Thursday. Are you well?'

'My goodness. You do get about.' She was already ruffled, bits of her flying off, a rag-bag. 'What about Wednesday then?'

'Very well, if you don't mind a quick lunch here in the office.'

'I'll take a quick lunch anywhere.'

'Shall we say one o'clock?'

'Yes, let's say that. 'Bye, Ralph.'

Poor old Ralph, she said to herself, knowing that he was anything but poor. The only way she could deal with large, powerful men was to scale them like a beetle and perch on the tops of their heads, forcing herself to look down. Still, the old Yid was made of money and as fond of Isabel as anyone had ever been, at least until the girl became morose. Maybe he had mellowed in his old age, become charitable. She was never easy when consciously deceiving herself, but in a crisis it was often necessary. The least Ralph could do was to lend her enough money to keep Isabel out of harm's way – and hers – until the next bout of despair.

*

Rebecca was still woman enough to want to look her best on the rare occasions when she went to London. The trouble was that she no longer had a best to look; the most that could be said for the ravaged face was that it had a healthy tan, and the least said about the rest of her the better. Why was it that women like the little Muspratt looked so smooth, so ordered? Why did their bodies fit so neatly into their clothes – for some reason Rebecca thought of the little Muspratt's clothes coming first, her body adjusting to them – and why did their minds slot in so neatly behind their eyes, showing no mechanism? Rebecca's one dress had a cigarette burn on the skirt; all her tights – she went through a whole bagful, stuffed in the cupboard for years – were laddered; she didn't have a pair of shoes that weren't scuffed and muddy and her handbag, into which generations of pens had leaked, seemed to contain eight plant labels, various bits of string, a pruning knife lost three months ago and a good handful of earth, apart from a bundle of notebooks, a dictionary of botanical names and an indecipherable collection of bills and letters. The little Muspratt's handbag would be good, worn leather, regularly dubbined, containing purse, cheque book, keys and possibly a tortoise-shell powder compact and comb. Rebecca looked dourly at her reflection in the mirror. She bared her big yellow teeth. Mrs bloody Muspratt had never been beautiful; like a stick or a stone, a modest fragment of nature, she had nothing to ruin.

Rebecca slapped make-up over the cracks – the same brand, probably the same jar that she had used ten years ago; certainly the same lipstick and mascara. The result, she knew, was appalling. She looked like a television comic in drag. She hit her hair with the brush, without subduing it. Liberal quantities of vintage Jolie Madame, a coat missing its top button, and she was ready. If she had gone in her old jeans and jacket, she would at least have felt alive; as it was she had the impression of being sticky and trussed, like a badly embalmed corpse. She took a last look at the roses in the front garden; they would have changed for ever by the evening. As the engine of her 1975 Morris hacked and spluttered and hacked again she kept up a commentary of obscenities, ending, as it finally clattered into life, with 'Jesus Christ! Why can't they leave me alone?' – meaning the entire population of her life, the clamorous years, the insistent demands of stifled voices. A group of Brig Boys came screaming round the bend on their motor bikes. She put her foot hard down on the accelerator and missed them by a couple of inches, swerving back to the left side of the lane and waving them out of the way like nuisances.

*

Ralph Herbert married Rebecca in 1948 partly for her beauty, partly for her talent, but largely because she was the only woman he had ever met who didn't bore him after the initial ceremonies of falling in love were over. As an international banker and a civilized man, these qualities were important to him. He had obstinately resisted his mother's wails and his father's despair and set out to prove that even a black sheep could maintain the family honour. For fifteen years they had managed, he thought, very well. Rebecca produced a son and a daughter, and though she hadn't been the kind of mother his parents expected, she continued to be beautiful, talented and entertaining. They lived as befitted wealthy people, though never ostentatiously. He collected ivories and Rebecca collected experience. They both worked hard, though with little apparent effort. Ralph junior and Rachel both went to Millfield and grew up as good, sensible children.

But when Ralph was in his early fifties things began to go wrong. Rebecca's beauty became unsuitable. She didn't so much age as suffer a kind of inner collapse; her bones corroded with grief, though God knows she had nothing to grieve about; her talent wavered and he had the distinct impression that their more intellectual friends no longer took her seriously – she was all too willing to be interviewed on trivial subjects, to sign petitions and march in protests, even to lend her name to a few hysterical outbursts from the feminist movement. Worst of all, she became predictable; her humour soured; her opinions became heavy; her temper deteriorated. Ralph, feeling that he was embarking on what should be his prime of life, was conscious of a weariness that could easily become despair. He liked to be comfortable. He needed the perquisites of hard work and wealth. He was at his most vulnerable when he met nineteen-year-old Priscilla, who thought it was all a shame. Rebecca, behaving extremely unreasonably, divorced him. It was the most upsetting time of his life. He married Priscilla.

But that hadn't worked out either. He had hoped for a dependent companion, a loyal pet, but five years of money and relative idleness so stimulated Priscilla's wits that by the sixth she was not only running her own boutique, but planning to expand into the prêt-à-porter market; from there, she told him with a dreamy look, she would branch out into household, wallpapers, moulded plastics. He saw very little of her towards the end of their marriage and had an uneasy feeling that by the time they were divorced she barely recognized him.

So, bruised and sorry, he had returned to the fold. Within two years he married Shirley, a forty-year-old widow with two clever schoolboy sons – an elegant, understanding woman of his own kind. He had never been so happy. He glowed. Ralph junior and Rachel had both married well. They were a credit to him. Ralph encountered Isabel occasionally, but was careful never to inquire too closely into her circumstances. Shirley kept a Birthday Book, and had written Isabel's name in it; perhaps, if she knew the girl's address, Shirley actually sent her birthday cards. Having been educated at Queen's College and assimilated a good deal of indigenous culture during her marriage to a minor British peer, Shirley also knew the suitable token for all her friends' wedding anniversaries and seemed to be frequently wrapping small, expensive gifts of cotton, leather, wood and wool. Ralph's father died unconsoled, but his mother sang a perpetual Nunc Dimittis, enjoying a real daughter at last. Priscilla was now a tycoon in her own right – no worries there. Rebecca was the only skeleton in the family cupboard and her occasional shuffling and clanking had to be dealt with firmly, in case she did further damage.

*

Rebecca went to the City by bus and sat among secretaries who eyed her curiously. Somebody said she was Mr Herbert's first wife. The others didn't believe it. Somebody else said she was Rebecca Broune, a famous writer. The others had never heard of Rebecca Broune. They were scrubbed young women in loose, mannish clothes and spoke in cultivated voices. When Ralph's personal assistant ushered Rebecca into his presence she smiled at him forgivingly, trying to show that she wouldn't hold Rebecca against him.

Rebecca and Ralph had not met for ten years. They were both, for different reasons, astounded, though neither of them showed it. Ralph had always been a handsome man, but uxoriousness had perfected him. As he came out from behind his desk and glided rather than walked across the enormous drawing room of his private office towards her, Rebecca felt a spasm of admiration and regret, cruel as a wet winter. His hair had been grey since he was a relatively young man; now it was silver, closely curled to his head, the hair of a Roman emperor; the noble nose and brown, watchful eyes were unchanged, but his face had become blander, less agitated by the desire to please. He was tall, and had never been slim; she knew that a considerable belly must be contained somewhere between the massive chest and spare hips, but there was little sign of it – his dark suit gave him the line and grace of an old race-horse, lovingly groomed. She smelled a forgotten perfume – frankincense, myhrr? – and recognized the flat gold cuff-links, the discreet ruby, the touch of a dry, sterilized hand. Her pride wavered. She was dilapidated, finished.

'Well, Ralph?' Her voice came out strident.

He smiled, as well he might. 'Well, Rebecca. Sherry? Or would you prefer something stronger?'

'Sherry's fine.'

'Dry or medium?'

'Oh, for heaven's sake, Ralph. Dry.'

He brought it to her and then, humiliating her with all this service, offered olives. She grappled in her handbag for a cigarette, but the silver box was opened before she had found one, the onyx table-lighter ready.

'Still smoking.' He shook his head, maddeningly paternal. 'It's not good for you.'

She couldn't bear this. There was a new ladder down the shin of her tights, good Cryck mud on the heel of her shoe. 'It's Isabel. She's ready to leave the hospital –'

'Hospital?' his eyebrows slightly raised.

'She tried to do herself in about six months ago. You didn't hear?'

'No.' He scooped a non-existent crumb off the polished tabletop. 'I'm sorry.'

'She needs a decent place to live, something to keep her going for a few months at least. Can you lend me five thousand?'

'And how would you propose to pay it back?'

'I probably wouldn't.'

He sighed, reaching for the bell. 'I haven't much time, I'm

afraid.' He was wearing silk socks, neatly gartered. 'You don't change, Rebecca, in some ways.'

As Rebecca endured the cold salmon and white Bordeaux, she knew that she was already defeated. She had long ago lost the equipment for this kind of skirmish. She didn't honestly believe – any more than Ralph did – that Isabel would keep going for a few months if given a decent place to live. She knew that she must offer Isabel a home – temporary, please God – and had known it ever since the phone call. But it was a try, at least, and if it had worked she could have covered the whole thing up and let it rot there. It wasn't going to work.

The cheese, the salad, the wild strawberries. 'Do you eat like this every day?'

'Why?' he asked, mildly surprised. 'You find it too heavy?'

'No. I thought men of your age were always on a diet.'

'I don't find it necessary.'

Coffee, brandy. 'I thought you were in a hurry, Ralph.'

He flicked open his gold watch, slipped it back into his waistcoat pocket. 'My appointment isn't until two-fifteen. I don't believe in hurrying, it upsets the digestion.'

'You never had an upset digestion in your life.'

'Perhaps not. Yours, then.'

He was so formal and yet, in a dreadful way, so familiar. They were not just an old divorced couple. He had moved back to his Hebrew origins, entrenched himself in law and legend; from this inviolable position he saw her, she felt, at a great distance, a trivial, despicable creature, physically repulsive and morally unsound. What seemed to her insulting was, to him, the most strenuous effort to be tolerant and even kind. But there would be no conciliation, no compromise.

At last, the ceremony over, he sat at his desk and became a figurehead.

'It's out of the question, Rebecca. I'm very sorry.'

'You wouldn't notice the difference,' she mumbled.

'That's hardly the point. What about you? You're a best-seller, very little to spend your money on.'

'Not any more. Anyway, I've retired. Dried up, if you want to know.' She tried her old endearing grin, knowing the result was ghastly.

'I'm sorry to hear that.' His hand hovered towards his watch chain. 'You must have Isabel to live with you, obviously.'

'And keep her on what? You'll have to put up the alimony, Ralph.'

He didn't even bother to answer that. 'Presumably she can get a job.'

'In Cryck? You don't know what you're talking about. Why don't you give her a job?'

He sighed patiently. Rebecca was beginning to tire him. 'She's not trained for anything, as far as I know. She's unreliable.'

'Well, then. You brought her up. What made her unreliable?'

'No, Rebecca,' he said quietly.

'I'm not asking you to *like* the girl. I'm not even asking you to see her, or buy her a meal. Just enough to keep her from turning on the gas, that's all.'

'I suggest you disconnect your gas supply,' he said with a faint smile.

'I don't have any. I cook on electricity.'

At least she had the last word, but it was no comfort. She demanded to use his telephone. With great courtesy he lifted the receiver, pressed a button, waited for the dialling tone and passed it to her as though on a silver salver. Then he retired, presumably to his bathroom, for she heard the discreet flush of a cistern, a running tap.

'Isabel's about somewhere,' the ward sister said. 'Probably in the games room. I can send someone to look, if you like.'

'Don't bother. Tell her I shall be coming to see her this afternoon. Rebecca Broune.'

'Are you a relative, Mrs Broune?'

'Her mother.' Rebecca blew smoke into the receiver,

scratching her crotch where the tights itched. 'I suppose you thought she didn't have one.'

When Ralph came back into the room she said defiantly, 'I'll have to go and see her. The hospital's miles away, you can stand me a taxi.'

'I'll see that you have a car,' he said. 'But I wonder if I could ask you to wait for it in the waiting room? It's almost two-fifteen. You'll find it quite comfortable. Plenty of magazines.' He ushered her out. The young women glanced at her as though she were garbage. His door closed silently. For the first time in many years Rebecca wanted to weep.

9

Finding Mrs Broune had gone out – presumably for some time, since the house was locked and there was no sign of her having been in the garden that morning – Phyllis hurried back to consult the Yellow Pages. Her memory had become in fact like a sieve, retaining large, often unwieldy incidents and letting the rest – important details like names, dates, why she had gone upstairs – fall through. She remembered that the handyman's name was Sherry, Skerry; she knew he had something to do with glass, an office job. Beyond that it was a gamble.

She had no idea there were such complexities in glass: safety, bevellers, fibre manufacturers, fibre reinforced plastics and moulders for fibre reinforced plastics, merchants, silverers, glaziers, half the county must be employed in glass. Frowning over her spectacles she went down the entries line by line: Bamfield Glass, Patio Doors, Louvres, Mirrors, Leaded Lights, While-U-Wait glass cutting – that was it. But for some reason one couldn't ring him up, he must be 'sought out', in Mrs Broune's curious phrase. The next thing was to find Bamfield on the map. She enjoyed using her initiative over such problems. Life had perhaps been a little dull in Surrey.

She changed her clothes for this expedition, not out of vanity, but because she was used to dressing suitably for every occasion and a cool summer frock and straw hat seemed suitable for this one. The complete operation took less than five minutes. She barely glanced in the mirror, having no need to reassure herself that she looked quite nice, which was the limit of her ambition in this respect. It was a beautiful day. She might do a little sight-seeing, the Abbey or a country house, one of the gardens that were open to the public at this time of year. Make a day of it. She missed Gerald of course, but occasionally there was something quite stimulating about being on one's own.

Remembering her visit to Mr Weaver, she stopped for lunch at Polly's Pantry in a small town where all the streets seemed to be named Sheep, Lamb, Ewe or Wool; but the only sign of this ancient trade was a range of dubious tartans and Shetland Knit behind bottle-glass windows, otherwise the place seemed to be given over to plastic. She wandered round for a while, looking for something to amuse Jasper and Selina, but there was nothing worth buying and she drove on, rehearsing what she would say to Mr Sherry or Skerry. It seemed a very long way for him to come, particularly if he had other work. Mrs Broune had said they wouldn't get on, and she still couldn't understand what that meant. She always got on with people, though clearly Mrs Broune didn't. It all depended on the right approach. She would know in an instant whether Sherry – Skerry? – was 'my good man' or 'Mister' or a more friendly Christian name; she would know what to pay him, what extras to provide, what degree of leniency she could afford without appearing soft. Perhaps he had done some jobs for Mrs Broune and not been properly appreciated. A little praise worked wonders, she had always found.

There was only one thing wrong with all this. It wasn't true. The glow of smugness faded, was replaced by perplexity. She had failed with Slattery. The tradesmen in Lamberts Heath didn't respect her. The Vicar hadn't called. She was ignored by the neighbourhood. Mr Weaver had behaved most strangely. Everything seemed to point to the fact that an old woman alone, without husband (or son) to support her, was a superfluous nuisance with no authority.

She felt a tremor of self-pity and doubt. Now come along, we can't have that. Cryck was not an easy village, the Brigadier seemed to have some sinister influence and his henchmen, the dreadful Boys, were enough to upset anyone. She had behaved impeccably, not letting them know by so much as a flicker how much they frightened her even after the outrageous attack on her field. She herself would think twice about visiting Cryck, if she didn't live there. It was all very unfortunate, but it wasn't her fault. It was her duty, in fact, to take a dignified stand; to civilize the place, if possible. She would get this Sherry or Skerry on her side and show them – the lot of them – that she was there to stay. Colour rose easily in her cheeks – always had, since she was a girl. It made her look much younger, in the prime of life.

The glass works took some finding. She parked with the trucks and lorries, locked her car and went into the low, sprawling building by the door marked Information. A pleasant man in brown overalls greeted her politely. There was carpet on the floor and samples of glass hung neatly on the blue wall.

'I'm looking for a Mr Sherry,' she said; then, with a confidential little laugh, 'Or is it Mr Skerry? I'm not quite sure.'

The man's expression changed, presumably because she was not going to order glass. He looked at her for a moment, then his grin broadened out of all proportion to her pleasantry. 'Fred Skerry,' he said.

'Thank you. Is he about, by any chance?'

'Oh, he's about.' He opened a frosted glass door behind the desk and bellowed, 'Jim! Tell Fred there's a lady to see him!' then closed the door again and leant on the desk, as though settling down to enjoy her company.

'Bin in these parts long, have you?'

'Well, no. Not these parts exactly. I live near Lamberts Heath.'

'Do you now. What part?'

'It's a village called Cryck. I haven't been there very long.'

'Oh, I know Cryck all right. Mrs Chalmers at the Old Rectory.'

'She died just before I moved in – such a pity, I would like to have known her.'

'Yes, very sad that. Who told you about Fred, then?'

'Mrs Broune, at Garden Cottage.'

'*Really*?' He seemed to relish each piece of information more than the last. 'You're a friend of hers, then?'

Before she could answer – just as well, because she didn't know how she would sum up her relationship with Rebecca – Fred Skerry came in. She was taken aback by his appearance, this being one of the things she hadn't anticipated. He was about fifty, she thought, tall and trim, with a clipped moustache and a clear blue eye, quite a gentleman. 'Fred Skerry,' he said, with a nice, firm handshake. 'Can I be of any assistance?'

She was quite flustered. The man in the brown overalls withdrew, muttering something about invoices. Skerry listened attentively while she told him about the bathroom, the draughts, the sockets. From time to time he nodded to indicate that he perfectly understood. 'And Mrs Broune told me,' she finished, 'that you sometimes – that you occasionally find time – to do a little extra work of this sort. Though it seems a dreadfully long way to go.'

'That's no problem – I live over that way.'

'Oh, do you?' A moment's doubt, a shy glance under the straw brim. 'Have you ... had any dealings with the Brigadier?'

'Wainwright? Wouldn't know him from Adam. Why do you ask?'

'Well, one gets the feeling that a lot of people ... It's rather an odd village.'

'Yes, so I've heard.' He smiled with kind eyes. 'Your husband doesn't go in for this sort of thing, I take it?'

'Oh – I'm so sorry – how silly of me. My husband died nearly three years ago. That's why I moved to Cryck, you see. He *was* very good at it, of course, that's probably why I ...' She decided not to finish that sentence, it was going too far. 'My name's Mrs Muspratt.'

'Well, Mrs Muspratt, if you're all alone we've got to help you out, haven't we?' He made it sound as though he were shouldering a delightful burden. 'Suppose I come over and have a look? I leave here at five. I'm afraid I'm busy this evening and tomorrow – can't let people down, you know – but how about Friday at seven?'

'Thank you very much, Mr Skerry. That would be excellent. It's Coachman's Cottage, the last house on the right at the bottom of the hill – a green gate, badly in need of a coat of paint, I'm afraid!'

He saw her to her car and directed her out into the road with sensible signals. What a very pleasant man. What could Rebecca possibly have meant about them not getting on? She decided to go straight home and not bother about the Abbey today, now she had something to look forward to.

*

She made a list of things she must ask him, headed by 'how much?' But it wasn't necessary. He went round the house like a surveyor, tapping and testing, examining the window frames, tracing the plumbing and the likely position of the electric cables, scratching little flakes of varnish off the beams, peering up the chimney, trying out fastenings and handles. 'Very nice,' he kept saying. 'Excellent condition. Very well done. You made an astute buy here, Mrs Muspratt, if I may say so.'

She beamed with satisfaction. She was proud of it. And to the same extent crestfallen when he shook his head and looked glum.

'You need an entirely new bathroom,' he said. 'It amazes me how some people live. I'm sure you like to soak, read a magazine, play the wireless, don't you?' She blushed, as though admitting it. In fact she was a person who got in, washed, and got out again, simple as that. 'I thought so. This,' he said firmly, glaring at the damp walls, the torn lino, the rusted mirror, 'is a pigsty.'

He suggested knocking down the wall between the bathroom and the passage. It would mean the bathroom opened straight into the kitchen, 'But why not? You're not likely to have the Health Inspector to stay, and it's a good deal more friendly.'

She liked his sense of humour, his air of competence. 'But

77

isn't that a very big job?' she asked diffidently. 'I mean, could you manage that alone?'

'No problem. It's practically falling down already. Then we could move the radiator here ... the basin and toilet here ... take that old plywood off the bath and turn it round here ... And you've got room for a washing machine.'

'But I don't have a washing machine.'

'Who knows? You might want one, and then—nowhere to put it. It's always a good idea to make provision for these things. Nice polystyrene tiles on the walls and ceiling, for insulation. Double glazing no problem. Cork tiles on the floor. Cover them with one of those fluffy nylon mats. Towel rail over the radiator here. A pine toilet seat, I think, don't you? So much warmer on the bottom. Pretty curtains – you can make them yourself, I'm sure. *Voilà*, Mrs Muspratt – your bathroom!'

She giggled, in spite of herself. 'But how much will all that cost?'

'I'll give you an estimate, of course. Well, is the bathroom the first thing on the agenda? Shall I measure up?' He assumed the posture of a man about to take rapid action, his eyes twinkling. 'Oh, very well,' she said, laughing. 'But I can't promise to accept the estimate, you know.'

'All's fair in love and war,' he said, 'and I have a strong feeling, Mrs Muspratt, that this isn't going to be war.'

He measured the bathroom, humming to himself in an absent-minded way.

'That's it, then. I'll report for duty Monday evening, about the same time.'

'But the estimate – ?'

'My dear Mrs Muspratt,' he said gently, 'if you don't approve the estimate you've got a lot of other jobs that need doing. I should hate to think you didn't trust me.'

'Of course I do, Mr Skerry –'

'Fred, please. We've got to be friends, you know.'

'Of course. Well, thank you. I – would you like a drink before you go?'

'No, no. Very kind of you, but my wife ... I get into real trouble if she smells so much as a beer.'

She hadn't thought of him having a wife, but of course a man like that wouldn't be a bachelor, even a widower would be unlikely. She felt a pang of envy. How nice to be expecting Fred home, ready to scold him if she smelt drink on his breath, ready to tease him. He had a very smart car, wonderfully clean and polished. She would ask him more about himself on Monday. As he said, they ought to be friends.

*

Fred Skerry, she learned, had joined the Army as a young man and spent the best years of his life in it, seeing the world. Then he had broken his back – some accident, he was vague about it, she thought it probably had something to do with reckless courage – and spent a year trussed down in a hospital bed. Not much use to the Army after that, so though they offered him an office job he came home, meaning to study accountancy or some such sedentary profession. Well, he never got around to that. He knew a lot about cars, and had been a car salesman for a while, but there were too many crooks for his liking. He'd worked for a big landscape-gardening firm – enjoyed that – and had been a traveller for a paperback company. He had even been a toast-master for a while, sent out to various do's by a smart employment agency. It wasn't hard to get by, if you were an all-rounder and played fair. He'd landed up in the accounts department of Bamfield Glass because they were a sound, family firm and he enjoyed living in the country. So did his wife, by the way. They hadn't got any children, which was the one thing he'd have liked different. They said women didn't feel fulfilled until they'd had children, but his wife seemed quite happy about it; men, he thought, needed children more.

He supposed he was an artist in a way – a very small way, of course. He had that kind of temperament. Never happy unless he was doing something with his hands, making something, fixing something. He was getting real pleasure out of turning this bathroom into a thing of beauty. He meant that. It was as though she had given him the opportunity to paint a picture or write a poem. That was why he did this kind of work – not for the money. Of course he didn't talk like this to everyone. Some people would think he was mad. Sometimes *he* thought he was mad, particularly when the old back started playing up.

This information didn't come all at once, but was spread out over the following week. He never stopped working, never sat about; it was Phyllis, towards the end of the week, when the dust and rubble of the demolished wall had been cleared away, who sat at the kitchen table sewing curtains, asking questions, laughing at his jokes with little neighs of amusement or – he was sometimes too absurd – schoolgirl splutters, as much as to say she didn't believe a word of it. He had never brought the estimate – 'I've got ways and means, Mrs M. – quite a few useful friends, you understand. Now if I wrote down a lot of figures and it ended up by not costing you half that – well, what's the point?' He arrived at seven, and always started tidying up at nine-fifteen, cleaning the bath so that she could use it, putting clean newspaper on the floor. He left at nine-thirty – 'I don't mind staying later,' he said the first evening, 'but I know you ladies – you like your beauty sleep' – and would never accept a drink or a cup of tea, let alone anything to eat. When he arrived and left he was as impeccable as on the afternoon they first met, but while he was working he wore an old sports shirt and overalls, flakes of plaster in his eyebrows and moustache. He naturally closed the door while he was washing and changing, and after she had remarked on the transformation one evening, he took to bursting out of the bathroom with a 'Ta-ra! Ta-ra!', striking a pose so that she could admire his magically changed appearance. All these things comforted her wonderfully.

10

Phyllis couldn't resist calling on Rebecca to tell her about the success of her search for a handyman. There had been something in the way Mrs Broune had suggested Fred and then so deliberately withdrawn the suggestion that made Phyllis feel she had scored a small triumph. *I get on with him very well,* she wanted to say, with a wealth of meaning. It was a little spiteful, perhaps, but after all, she was Michael's mother, in a very roundabout way you might even say that Rebecca Broune was dependent on her goodwill. Anyway, she was pleased with her news and rather hoped Rebecca wouldn't be.

She found Rebecca spraying a rose bed and would have been appalled had she known the extent of Rebecca's fury at being interrupted; she was very near to being physically assaulted for impertinence and trespass.

'Jeyes Fluid,' Rebecca said, giving one last savage pump. 'It's all I use. I suppose you believe in chemicals.'

'I'm afraid I don't know much about it, really. Gerald used a lot of different things, I know.'

Rebecca glared at her from behind her dark glasses. She was looking remarkably perky, damn her. Why does she pester me, this idiotic little creature with her Gerald, her meaningless simper, her beastly cardigan? It wasn't even time for a drink.

'What d'you want? Tea?'

'No – please – I was just passing, I don't want to –'

'You might as well have some tea, since you're here.' She stormed off down the path, leaving Phyllis to follow.

'I came last week,' Phyllis said, when the mug had been dumped in front of her. 'Wednesday, I think it was, but you were out. I wanted to ask –'

'I had to go to London,' Rebecca said. 'I do, occasionally, go out.'

'Yes, of course. I simply wanted to ask you –'

She might as well pay for her intrusion. 'I went to see my daughter in the bin.'

'In the – ?'

'Bin. Loony bin. Asylum. Mental hospital. What do *you* call it?'

'Oh. I'm so sorry. Is she – ?'

'As well as can be expected after filling herself with gas and a bottle of phenobarbitone. What did you want to ask?' She was devouring, rather than smoking, her cigarette. She looked so unhappy, or angry, or both, that Phyllis was alarmed for her. It was not the right time to bring up her own problems. She was very reluctant to know about Mrs Broune's, which were certain to be distressing, but courtesy required her to ask, 'Will she be there long?'

'They're letting her out at the end of the week. She's coming here.'

'That's nice,' Phyllis said. 'Much the best thing, I'm sure. You'll be able to take care of her.' She knew she was talking at random, but there was something about Mrs Broune that made her feel as though she were hearing great passions sung in Italian or watching wars on television; one didn't know what all the fuss was about and yet undoubtedly there was fuss. 'Is she quite . . . better?'

There were half a dozen answers to that. No, she'll never be better. Better than what? What is 'better'? Did the woman have a clear idea of 'best'? Yes, she probably did: best behaviour, all for the best. Since seeing Ralph, and Isabel so locked in her own concerns that she couldn't even look up, couldn't loosen her grip on her own arms or uncross her legs, Rebecca had felt an urgent longing to speak, to make herself heard. What she wanted to say, beyond asserting her existence, she didn't know. What was there to say? For most of her life, she had commanded attention; now she couldn't even command her own. The need to tell, express, confess, produced nothing but mumbled platitudes and petulant complaints. She felt hollow, except for the sensation of being hollow.

For a moment she contemplated shocking the little Muspratt by telling her that she couldn't stand Isabel, that the prospect of having Isabel to stay was an assault, a threat, an outrage. But what, after all, was the point? So she simply said, 'Yes. She's better,' and let the silence fall like a lid.

But little Mrs Jack-in-the-box wasn't having that. 'What's her name? Is she married? How old is she? Just a year younger than Sophia, of course Sophia's married and has two lovely children. It sounds a terrible thing to say, but you know I rather envy you. Not the worry, of course, but having your daughter all to yourself for a little while. That seems impossible once they have a family. I suppose one's meant to – well, you know, put the grandchildren in their place, as it were, and of course I adore them, but one's children are always, well, one's children, aren't they? They always come first.'

Rebecca was amazed how easily the words flowed and how precisely they depicted little Muspratt's feelings. She was even more amazed at the woman's apparently unquestioning assumption that what she had to say was of the slightest interest. It was an enviable egotism bestowed on the dreariest people. She, Rebecca, had lost hers in the echoing lacunas of self. To offer more than a few dry sticks of information was impossible for her.

'You wanted to ask me something,' she said.

'Yes, I wanted to ask you where I could find Fred Skerry – the handyman. I'd forgotten what you said – really, I should write everything down! Anyway, I found him all right in the end, and I just wanted to thank you –'

'You've taken him on?'

'Yes, he seems most efficient, and such a friendly man.'

Rebecca smiled, which was nice to see, but didn't say anything. She ground her cigarette into the ashtray. The sun glasses were enigmatic.

'I'm rather puzzled,' Phyllis said lightly, 'by you saying we wouldn't get on. He's so polite and helpful.'

'Did I say that?' Disappointingly, after the smile, her voice was bleak. 'Oh. Well. I say things. Fred's all right. I hear you had some trouble with the Brig Boys?'

Phyllis hesitated. No, she wasn't going to give Rebecca the satisfaction of being right. 'Nothing very much,' she said. 'Just a little misunderstanding, quite easy to deal with really.'

Rebecca walked with her to the gate. She seemed preoccupied, sad, almost meek. Phyllis decided she needed cheering up. 'I told Michael I knew you – he was most impressed.'

'Michael? Oh, your publisher son.'

'I'd love to be able to tell him what you're working on now – or is it a Dire Secret?' She twinkled mischievously.

'Good God!' Rebecca roared. 'I work in the garden! Can't you *see*?'

She really was very difficult. No wonder her daughter was – well, odd. Phyllis felt decidedly put out as she hurried away. She would keep her distance in future – or at least until Michael could spare time for a visit. She didn't feel so alone any more, for some reason.

'Do we have Rebecca Broune?' Michael asked Piers, his new assistant.

'Who?' Piers' eyes always looked as though they were trying to get out through the impenetrable lenses of his spectacles; they swam about, frantically bumping against the glass. He was an unattractive youth, but clever.

'Broune. Rebecca. Notable lady novelist. Before your time, perhaps, but so was Jane Austen.'

Piers winced. 'Perhaps she's in the cellar.'

'Perhaps she is, but could you be good enough to go and look?' As the young man floundered through the door, even more ungainly on his feet, Michael called out, 'B-r-o-u-n-e. Not like Ford Madox.'

'Like who?'

Michael made a weary gesture, signifying it didn't matter. Piers flapped off down the corridor. It was late in the afternoon. The chestnuts in the square were at their best, not yet dusty with summer. A small boy rattled a stick along the bumpers of parked cars. An old man sat on a bench reading a book. A girl with cerise hair waited at the pedestrian crossing. The traffic stopped and she picked her way over the road like a plover. The traffic moved again, the afternoon continued.

'They weren't in the cellar,' Piers said. 'They were under the stairs.'

'What?' Michael was momentarily bewildered, as though he had been sleeping. 'Oh. The Brounes. Thanks, Piers.'

Piers scanned the titles of the three books he was holding. 'Any good?' he asked.

'So they say. I don't know. I've never read them.' He reached for the books. 'Thanks, Piers.'

Piers was reading the backs of the jackets. He tucked two of the books under his arm and read through the blurb inside the other. Michael waited, resting his elbow on the desk but still holding out his hand. Meanwhile, he thought of other things.

'What do you want them for?' Piers asked vaguely.

'To read, Piers. To *read*.'

'Oh.' The young man shoved them at him clumsily. 'Sorry. Should I have heard of her?'

'Oh yes, you should have *heard* of her, Piers. You should have heard of obscure pre-Raphaelite painters and Cornelius Cardew. Whether you should actually study such things is another matter. Is this all there were?'

'I think so.'

'Then the rest must be in the cellar. Have a look some time.' He shrugged on his jacket, picked up the books and made for the door. Some peculiar impulse – a need somehow to prove that Piers was real – made him ruffle the boy's hair as he passed. Piers goggled. Michael smiled amiably. 'Thanks, Piers,' he said.

*

Michael remembered seeing Rebecca Broune at the launching of one of her novels about twelve years ago – perhaps the last book she had written, he couldn't be sure. He hadn't been introduced to her, being very junior in those days and not particularly interested; he remembered thinking she looked more like an out-of-work actress than a writer, a lot of make-up, black velvet and despair. All his contemporaries had read her, but he disliked twentieth-century women novelists, including Mrs Woolf who, in his opinion, would have been far better employed as a schoolteacher. They were either soft-centred bitches or malicious slobs – his vocabulary at the time – and he had no sympathy with their view of the world.

He still didn't care for them, though he had learned not to admit it. People in a state of transition – women, adolescents, transexuals, invalids, restless coal miners and most blacks – shouldn't write novels. Their books were messages from chaos. He believed that the purpose of fiction was to observe without judgement; all these categories – but particularly women – judged without observation. They had nothing to offer but prejudice and self-pity. Privately, he believed that the Brontës and Austens and Eliots were an extinct breed, irresponsibly slaughtered by a bunch of self-conscious schoolgirls. He had few hopes of Rebecca Broune, but he was interested to try and find out why she had stopped writing. It showed, he thought, an unusual fastidiousness in a successful author.

He was not, for once, going out that evening. He glanced at his mail – letters from friends, postcards from god-children, advance programmes from the Festival Hall and B.B.C. – and made a couple of phone calls. He put Saint-Saëns' Violin Concerto on the record player, listened for a couple of minutes then changed it for the Mozart F Major Oboe Quartet. He wandered about, silently whistling along with Goossens, beating time with pursed fingers, pausing in the slow passages to stare out of the window without looking. Music helped him suspend his identity, to return to his natural state after a day of compromise. His friends said that music was his great passion, but he was unaware of passion. He didn't actually think about music at all, any more than he thought about the surrounding air; they were both, and for the same purpose, necessary.

When the Quartet was over he switched to Radio 3 and was briefly offended by an American lecturing on structural linguistics. Nothing else for it, then. He opened a bottle of wine and settled himself in an armchair by the window, feet and the novels of Rebecca Broune on the coffee table, telephone on the floor within reach. But he made no attempt to start reading. He was almost happy. When the phone rang he stretched for the receiver automatically, without changing his mind.

'It's Sophia. That was very quick.'

'Oh – Sophia.' He liked his sister, but they seldom saw each other nowadays, and never spoke on the telephone without reason. 'How are you?'

'Fine. Just got your nephew and niece into bed, thank God.'

'Are they all right?'

'They're fine.'

'And Bron?'

'He's fine. I wondered if you were thinking of going to see Mother at all.'

'Mother. Why? Isn't she well?'

'She's perfectly *well*, Mike, as far as I know. It's just that you haven't been and I can't at the moment with the kids and all, and – well, I just think it would be nice if you could. That's all.'

'I see.' He reached for the top book and looked at the photograph on the back cover – not promising. 'Did she ask you to ask me?'

'Of course not. She's asked you herself plenty of times. She says you're always busy.'

'Well. I have been busy.'

'Please, Mike. Make an effort.'

He hadn't heard that note in Sophia's voice before. He tended to think of her as a small girl, or anyway a girl, always busy with private concerns. She was, of course, a middle-aged woman. 'All right,' he said. 'I'll go when I can.'

'No panic. You know, it's just –'

'The weekend after next,' he said. 'How's that?'

'Thanks. Will you tell her?'

'I shan't just arrive unannounced, if that's what you mean.'

'No, don't do that. You might find her in bed with her new handyman.'

'*What?*'

'A joke, dear. Sorry. No, she's found this fellow who's fixing up the house for her. She thinks he's wonderful. Quite girlish she sounds.'

'You don't honestly think – ?'

'Of course not. Are you married yet?'

'No. Aren't you divorced yet?'

88

There was a moment's silence; a mere pause, but it gaped.
'Not quite. Shall we see you some time?'
'Of course. Very soon.'
'Take care, then.'
'And you.'
Michael's evening had been disturbed. Sophia didn't sound happy. His women friends, most of them Sophia's sort of age and – he supposed – type, would have poured it all out. But Sophia had always been reticent with him, perhaps inhibited, as he was, by family relationship. He would be unable to help or comfort her for the same reason, though he was renowned among his friends for being a help and comfort. Just as he couldn't be his mother's handyman, though perfectly capable of drilling and plugging walls, painting nurseries and unblocking drains for other people. Odd, that. He decided to eat some Stilton and listen to Haydn.

While he did so, he unwillingly considered the problem of visiting Cryck. He hadn't seen Phyllis much – as much as he should? – since she had been a widow and, apart from that once when he had taken her out to lunch, always at home in familiar surroundings. He dreaded having to admire or criticize or have any opinion at all about what he supposed was her new home; he dreaded having to find his way about; above all he dreaded the inevitable ceremony, the meals, the serving and cosseting as though he were a man of substance. He enjoyed spending his weekends with families and small groups of friends with whom he could play a minor role; he relished the extra chair or stool at the corner of the table, the camp-beds and sofas, the way he was so naturally included and overlooked. For that first, agonizing meal after his father died, Phyllis had put him at the head of the table. He had moved the mat – Audubon birds, were they? – and cutlery back to his usual place opposite Sophia. There was no usual place for him – yet – in her new surroundings, and she might well repeat the blunder. In fact she had probably already designated the wingchair, Gerald's tankard and napkin ring (Phyllis still used napkin rings), a bathroom shelf and a couple of coat-hooks downstairs for his constant use. Any walk he might take, any preference he might express, even the time he went to bed and the time he got up, would be in danger of becoming usual. He couldn't live up to that. He loved her – he assumed, in so far as he was able – but it was never intended that he should be an important part of her life, let alone – God forbid – the most important.

He settled once more by the window, adjusting the lamp, propping his feet up, trying to recapture his earlier contentment. At least she'd found this fellow. That was a relief. He chose one of the Broune novels at random, sighed deeply and began reading.

Anyone watching Michael – the window was open until midnight, the curtains remained undrawn, the lamp sang with midges – would have seen him look up occasionally from the book, scratch his head, rub his eyes, yawn, pour another glass of wine, return to the book again; sometimes he got up, disappeared, leaving the open book face down over the arm of the chair, came back zipping his fly, flopped down and continued reading. Once or twice he raised his head and would have appeared to be staring at someone on the other side of the room. Once he flung the book down and sprawled, hands holding the back of the chair but head invisibly sunk, for at least five minutes; then doggedly picked up another. An observer would have been bored by this time. Unobserved, Michael went on reading.

It was dawn by the time he threw the last book down and stretched and exercised his face and got up, peered blearily out of the window, shuffled across the room towards bed. He paused at his desk, took a card out of the rack and, without sitting down, scribbled, 'Dearest Mother – How about the weekend of the 25th? Can't get down before. Will arrive about 12 unless I hear from you. Would be interested to meet R. Broune if she's about. Don't bother to confirm. Love, Michael.'

'Fred . . . ?'

He was up the step-ladder in the bathroom, fixing polystyrene on the ceiling. He smiled down at her. 'Madame?'

'My son's coming for the weekend on the 25th. That's the week after next. Will you have finished by then?' A flicker seemed to cross his face, as though he were wounded. She said quickly, 'The bathroom, I mean.'

'It'll be finished by Wednesday,' he said. 'Mind you, I can't promise the same for the curtains and whatnots *which* somebody seems to be taking her time about.'

'I know. I'm sorry. I'll get them done, really. But it's the floor in the spare-room – there seems to be a large hole, and I'm afraid if I move the bed –'

'Down will come sonny, cradle and all. Well, we can't have that, can we?' He laboriously descended the steps and suddenly made an exclamation of pain, clutching the small of his back. 'Bloody back,' he said. 'Sorry, Mrs M. It's the stretching.'

'It's the moving that bath,' she said, with asperity. 'I told you not to do it alone. We could have found somebody.'

'Yes, mam. You're right, mam.' He saluted, standing to attention. She could imagine him making a joke even in front of a firing squad. 'Well now – where's this hole of yours?'

The door at the bottom of the stairs was difficult to open, she often had to tug at it three or four times. Fred opened it for her and gave it a quick inspection. 'Hm,' he said. 'Needs a new ball catch. Have to see to that.' He followed her up the dark spiral. She was hauling herself up by holding the rope that was fixed at intervals down the wall – one of Jack Sanderson's clever ideas – and suddenly slipped on one of the worn treads. Still clinging to the rope, she swung back on Fred's protective hands. 'Whoops!' he said, righting her.

'Mind how you go. These stairs are a proper deathtrap, and that rope's frayed. *I* don't know, Mrs M. You need a body-guard, that's what you need.'

Blushing, disconcerted – what on earth could be the matter with her? – Phyllis showed him into the spare-room. The double bed – she had brought that in case Sophia and Bron came to stay, or Michael and some impossible to imagine future wife – filled up most of the room. She had pushed it a little to one side while making it up and there – she indicated it helplessly – was this hole.

Fred lowered himself cautiously to the floor and peered under the bed. He thumped the floorboards with his clenched fist and groped with one hand in the hole, squinting up at her with a look of concentration. 'No problem,' he said. 'I'll patch it up for you. Sonny'll be quite safe.' He got up, groaning, and fell prostrate on the bed, grabbing at his back in agony.

'Oh, Fred – are you all right?' A foolish question, since he so obviously wasn't, but the first that entered her head.

'Only thing to do,' he gasped, 'give it a massage.' He rolled over on his stomach, plucking at the straps of his overalls.

'But I don't know how to –'

'Just gently.' His face was screwed up like a small boy's. He was having such difficulty with the overalls that she felt bound to help him. When they had both, with effort, got the overalls round his knees, revealing much nattier underpants than Gerald had ever worn, he pulled up his shirt and feebly pointed at the base of his spine. 'Just there.' His face cleared, as though expecting benison.

She approached him cautiously. She had never touched any man but Gerald, and that had been a long time ago (and then he had been dead). The shadow between Fred's buttocks – surprisingly plump they were, for so spare a man – worried her. She laid her hands flat on the white skin and pressed until she felt bone; then she stroked with a deep, circular move-ment, as she had done the children's stomachs when they were constipated.

'Ah . . .' Fred sighed. 'That's better. Use your thumbs, Mrs M., the thumbs.'

With her thumbs she found his knobbly coccyx and kneaded it, looking at him anxiously for signs of relief.

'Harder,' he breathed. 'Lower.'

She withdrew. Something – she didn't know what it was – repelled her. The competent, comical Fred had become passive, shameless as a bitch in heat. She didn't like it at all. She stood up, thrusting her hands into her cardigan pockets.

'Is it any better?' she asked sharply.

He seemed to hesitate, then opened one bright eye, almost mocking her. 'Much better, Mrs M.' He heaved himself round, climbed slowly off the bed, pulled up his overalls and fastened the straps. 'You've got just the right touch. With practice, you could set up quite a little business.'

She glared at him. He smiled back, friendly, innocent, grateful. 'I'm much obliged to you,' he said, without irony. 'It won't happen again.'

Although she tried to make light of it, she was uneasy for the rest of the evening. He went on with the bathroom ceiling, humming to himself, sometimes breaking into a few bars of song. She did a little dead-heading in the garden, then walked down to the stream. The cows, back from milking, were standing in a symmetrical pattern over by the willows. Did this mean rain or shine? She missed her usual evening gossip with Fred, but didn't want to go back indoors while he was there. She wanted to ask him what the cows were predicting – he would certainly know – and was impatient with herself for feeling turned out of her own house. It was all very unfortunate. She didn't know what to think.

The back door opened and there he was, silhouetted in the bright doorway, properly dressed and searching for her.

'Mrs M. . . . ?'

She kept quiet, hiding in the twilight at the bottom of the field.

'Good night, then,' he called mournfully. 'See you tomorrow ...'

'Good night, Fred.' She had raised her voice, but knew he couldn't hear her. The back door closed, and in a few minutes she heard his car starting up. The headlamps swept up the hill. She walked slowly back to the house, hugging herself against the cold.

He had left a note on the kitchen table: 'Will bring flrbrds tomorrow – sorry about the mess – Take care – FS'. Really, I'm ridiculous! A real old woman! She urgently needed a restorative and suddenly thought of pouring herself a small brandy. She had never done such a thing before, not even when Gerald died. It made her feel much more worldly. You're nothing but an old prude. The poor man was really suffering. How could she have been so callous, so dreadfully silly? She wished she could ring him up and apologize, but had no idea where he lived. 'I'm thoroughly ashamed of myself,' she wanted to say. 'Please forgive me, Fred.' She went to bed rather unsteadily, hiccoughing and humble.

The next morning she felt much calmer. Better not to apologize, after all. Better simply to ignore the incident. She was still very disturbed by her reaction – Rebecca Broune, a sophisticated woman, she supposed, would have despised her for it. Which reminded her that Michael was coming – somehow that had gone out of her head last night – and that Rebecca must be persuaded to meet him. She wouldn't say anything about the incident of Fred's back, of course – but it would be nice to think that if she did, it might make a light, amusing story, showing her own savoir-faire, not to mention sympathetic nature – something which Rebecca Broune certainly couldn't boast about. She was going to put the brandy bottle back in the cupboard when she thought no, why should I? She poured the brandy into a cut-glass decanter – thank goodness she'd kept one – and put it on top of her mahogany sewing box. Then she brought out the whisky and sherry – no decanter for that, she must buy one – and displayed them too, adding four good glasses, placed upside down, a bottle opener and a corkscrew. That was much better. She felt she had grown up considerably in the last twelve hours.

She wrote a note to Rebecca simply asking her to come for a meal on the 25th, not mentioning Michael. 'Please don't bother to change,' she scribbled, 'it's *most* informal! And do of course bring your daughter.' The prospect of Rebecca in her filthy denims and sunglasses, accompanied by a mentally deficient – well, disturbed – daughter was not encouraging, but it would be gratifying to introduce Michael to one of his authors and she felt much more able to cope with it now. She nipped up to the post box and spent much of the afternoon planning a menu. The possibility that Rebecca would refuse the invitation must be dealt with if it arose; she had a feeling that her note had a certain tone of authority.

After tea she changed into an almost new pair of trousers – slacks, she called them – that Sophia had given her after Selina was born. Sophia couldn't get into them, she said, and since Phyllis was so tiny she might as well have them. Phyllis had never dreamt of wearing them – they were unsuitably close-fitting and not at all her style – but in her new boldness decided to try them on, and thought that with her cashmere twinset they really looked quite ... stylish. A touch of pale lipstick and she was moderately pleased with herself. It must be sad to look as – well, dilapidated as Mrs Broune. Poor thing. She busied herself with the bathroom curtains, expertly guiding the foot of her sewing machine along the Rufflette, snipping the cotton and threading the needle and snipping the cotton. Her heart felt lighter than it had done for years.

She had expected Fred might look a little sheepish or, worse, offended when he came. But not a bit of it. He arrived with an armful of floorboards, an impression of Christmas in spite of the June weather. 'Top of the evenin' to you, Mrs M. Managed to get some seasoned elm for you, just the job.' He manoeuvred across the room, she hurried to open the stairs door for him, tugging at it ineffectually for a few moments.

'Must remember that ball catch,' he muttered, easing the planks into the stairwell and lifting them step by step to the landing. 'Can you manage?' she asked. 'Can I help?' He came down brushing his hands together. 'I'll get on with that,' he said, 'if that's what you'd like. I could have got tongue 'n groove but I thought no, she's proud of her little cottage and I don't think a few pounds here or there is going to bother her much.'

She agreed anxiously. He went into the bathroom and closed the door. When he came out in his overalls, she held up one of the curtains and said, 'Finished, you see,' with pride.

'That's my girl. Very pretty, too.' He grinned, almost bashfully. 'Like yourself, Mrs M., if you don't mind my saying so.'

She sat down at the sewing machine again, putting on her spectacles and fussing to hide her pleasure. He went upstairs and hammered and sawed all evening. Flakes of plaster fell off the ceiling and sometimes she looked up at it, alarmed, thinking how difficult it must be for him to work with that bed in the way and it couldn't be doing his back any good. But she stayed downstairs.

At nine-fifteen he came down with his tools, a dustpan full of sawdust and a bagful of shavings, which he emptied into the grate. 'There you are,' he said. 'Safe as houses. I'll just wash up, then I'll be off.'

Was he being just a little stand-offish? Perhaps working up there had reminded him, perhaps he'd been puzzling about her behaviour while his back ached in that cramped space. What could she do to make amends, without actually saying anything? At twenty-five minutes past nine, when he appeared with his 'Ta-ra! Ta-ra!' – she was grateful for it, but what could he have thought last night, when she had deserted him? – she said timidly, 'I was just going to have a nightcap – I do wish you'd join me. It's not right, you know, to drink alone.'

He looked dubious. 'What about the wife?' he asked. But he was smiling.

'I'm sure she wouldn't object. Tell her you had to – out of politeness to me.'

'Oh, well, then. If you put it like that. A small Scotch would come in very handy, Phil.'

She stiffened, in spite of herself. That wasn't necessary. That was going too far. They were much too close in the kitchen. She could smell the soap he had washed with, and a strong undersmell of sweat. She picked up the drinks tray. 'It's such a lovely evening – let's go outside. I like to sit outside for a little while before going to bed.'

'Do you now?' He took the tray from her and stood to one side to let her through the door. 'I'm getting to know quite a lot of your little habits. Very nice they are, too.'

He refused ice and got his own water from the kitchen tap. They settled themselves on either side of the garden table. Gnats swam in the shaft of light from the back door. He lit a small cigar, after asking her permission.

'Well,' he sighed. 'This is really very pleasant.'

She smiled, sipping her brandy delicately. They didn't talk much. He left at ten o'clock, taking the tray indoors with him. She sat on for a while in the warm garden, greatly reassured.

Rebecca had been up since five. She had watched the slow crescendo of light, ash to pearl, pearl to rose, rose to sapphire. Her hair warmed first, like a mat; then her left cheek, her arm, her bare leg with its knobbly shin and knotted veins. The new moon hung in sunlight. The air, which had moved a little during the night, settled. If a bird moved from twig to twig there was a commotion. Rebecca valued this time of day more than any other. She submitted to it, letting her coffee cool, exhaling smoke which drifted of its own volition towards the garden. Though she was not aware of it, her face rested during these early hours and became the face of a very old child.

She had dreaded Isabel being an early riser, but thank God the girl always slept late. The first assault of the day usually came from the postman. This morning she heard the snap of the letter box but delayed going indoors – there would certainly be something to enrage or depress her and she clung, every morning, to her short ration of peace. Finally she shuffled in and picked up the letters from the floor, peering at them through her one fully open eye.

Phyllis's card was, of course, an outrage. Of course, without question, she would refuse. To waste an entire evening having 'conversation' (Rebecca always thought of conversation in quotation marks, believing it to be a myth concocted by biographers of nineteenth-century poets) in somebody else's house, or worse, in somebody else's garden, was one of her ideas of hell. She had many ideas of hell; the one thing they had in common was other people. It was typical of the little Muspratt to come barging in where even her friends feared to tread. Her friends were not conspicuous by their presence; indeed, she doubted whether she had any; if she had, little Muspratt was perfectly welcome to join them in oblivion.

She leafed through the rest of the post for cheques – there were none – and threw the letters unopened on the table, from where they would later join the tottering pile of rubbish on her desk. She bathed quickly, still fuming against Phyllis, and dropped a voluminous smock over her naked old body. There was a lot to do – straw down the strawberries, prune the currants, plant out the sweet corn and tomatoes, cut down delphiniums, take cuttings of Mrs Sinkins, sow some more morning glory and dill, scythe the bank, a couple of hours' watering this evening ... The thought that Isabel would need something to eat infuriated her further. The girl wasn't supposed to drive; she was dizzy with pills. There must be some bread and a bit of cheese in the fridge. There was plenty of lettuce, anyway, and peas if she could concentrate enough to pick them. No good asking her to plant out the leeks, I suppose. No good asking her to do anything. Isabel drifted ghostly through the days, an inaudible reprimand.

Rebecca's spirit leapt into the garden like a fish into water; her body plodded, carrying heavy weights. She glanced up at the drawn curtains, the shut window, of her daughter's bedroom and wondered impatiently where she had learned such stuffy habits. Then she decided to forget her.

But the decision didn't work. Whenever she looked towards the house the shut, curtained window was still there. Responsibility nagged. There was no one to share it. The hospital had informed Dr Martin in Lamberts Heath, but he obviously didn't understand a word of the letter and wouldn't believe it if he had. In Rebecca's opinion Martin might have made a sympathetic vet, but where anything more complex than constipation or bunions were concerned his ignorance was almost miraculous. He looked as though he should be grafted to a horse. He had passed on the hospital's letter to his dispenser, an elderly woman who could look things up, and told Isabel to take plenty of exercise, though since she didn't ride he wasn't sure how this could be done. Walks, perhaps. Tennis. Swimming. The consultation had produced nothing but extreme bewilderment in both doctor and patient. There was no point in repeating it.

Where then, Rebecca asked herself, tucking in strawberries, could she turn? Ralph was a dead loss. As far as she could tell, Isabel had no friends. Her life couldn't have been entirely unpopulated – at her age Rebecca herself had been struggling in a web of acquaintances and lovers – but there hadn't been so much as a postcard or phone call. The ward sister had told her – Rebecca realized that as Isabel's mother she was expected to react in some way to the information – that Isabel had received very few visitors. Well, very few was better than none at all. Where were they? Who were they? It was appalling that at this stage in her life she should be landed with a helpless infant. Even worse that the helpless infant should be thirty-five years old and extremely plain.

Her own isolation was, under the circumstances, a great disadvantage. If nobody wished or dared to approach Rebecca Broune, they certainly weren't going to take pity on her daughter. She mentally scoured the neighbourhood. Pip Chalmers had been a pleasant woman, very independent and easy to get on with, but she was dead. Emma Sanderson would have been a great help but ... Wait a minute. Rebecca, squatting in the strawberry bed, was struck with hope. What better occupation for the little Muspratt than to mother an unwanted child? She would do it out of spite, of course. It would look like a Muspratt triumph. So much the better. It would leave her, Rebecca, free to get on with her demanding work with less interruption, and it would give the little Muspratt much smug satisfaction. She might even cook. She had offered to cook already, for Christ's sake.

Well, if there was a chance of getting Isabel off her hands, she would take her to supper. It might be her own salvation, if not Isabel's. She hurried indoors and dashed off a card – a telephone call would be too much of a confrontation. 'Love to,' she wrote, signing it with an indecipherable scrawl. Isabel could take it to the box – at least she could do that much.

She was planting out the tomatoes, carefully tying them with soft string to their canes, when she saw the shadow come out of the back door and waveringly settle in the chair she herself had been sitting in earlier. It was almost noon, and very hot. Sweat was pouring unhindered inside her smock and she had been telling herself for half an hour that she needed her hat. She got up, groaning, and limped to the house.

Isabel watched her mother approach with a familiar sense of doom. When she finally arrived after this arduous journey up the path, she would certainly inflict some punishment. 'How did you sleep?' she might ask, inferring that it was Isabel's duty to sleep soundly; 'Have you had breakfast?', implying that if she hadn't, she was deliberately starving herself to annoy; worst of all would be 'How do you feel?', a question so unanswerable that to ask it was a deliberate gibe. She tensed herself, thin arms tightening round her knees. Rebecca lumbered up the steps, wiping her forehead with the back of her hand.

'How did you sleep?' It was, after all, a form of greeting.

'Quite well, thank you.'

'Have you had breakfast?' There was probably nothing to have, but it showed concern of a sort.

'I don't want any, thanks.' A pause. Then, unwillingly, 'I had some coffee.'

'Good, good,' Rebecca said vaguely. 'How do you feel?'

'All right, thanks.'

Rebecca sat down with a great puff of heat and exhaustion. She pulled the low neck of her smock away from her sticky skin and blew down it, noting with disgust the wrinkled, glistening breasts and belly. 'Hot today,' she said.

'Yes.'

They eyed each other warily, with flickering glances. Isabel, Rebecca thought, was quite unnecessarily drab. Her mouse-coloured hair hung over her extinguished face; her childish body was enveloped in some sort of khaki garment, a giant shirt perhaps, or instant shroud; her long, meagre feet were etiolated, sickly. What could you do with such an unsuccessful creature, except start again? Isabel, thinking herself camouflaged in the shade of the plum tree, imagined her mother as an old dog, scarred and moth-eaten, its yellow teeth still able to tear flesh, its hydrophobic little eyes like red-hot cinders in dark places. Her fear of her mother came out in her voice as cool indifference, each remark having an upward inflection to protect it.

'I'd like you to go to the post box for me, if you would,' Rebecca said.

'All right. Where is it?'

'You went there the other day.'

'Oh. Yes. Where those men are.' There was a long pause and then, coldly, 'I'd rather not.'

'Because of the Brig Boys?'

Isabel looked puzzled. 'No. The men.'

'Were they' – Rebecca searched wildly for a word – 'insolent?'

'I'd rather not go there.'

Another silence. Isabel bent over her toenails, pulling at dry skin.

'Very well,' Rebecca said, as though undertaking an onerous task. 'I'll phone her.'

Isabel didn't ask phone who. Her shoulders moved in a kind of shrug, as though she would like to have said 'That's your problem'. She continued to pick her toenails. 'Mrs Muspratt has asked us to supper on Saturday,' Rebecca burst out. 'I've written her a postcard saying we'll go.'

In the inevitable silence she heard exactly what Isabel was going to say. She knew Isabel was right. She was already thinking of her answer.

'You didn't ask me,' Isabel said on cue, without rancour but without life.

'I didn't think there was much point. Apart from the Brig Boys you seem to be quite indifferent to everything.'

Isabel covered her feet with the hem of her skirt, shirt or

whatever it was. She pulled it taut so that she appeared like a legless woman in a bag. She lowered her head between the encircling arms and sat motionless.

'I'll phone her,' Rebecca said, getting up. She waited for a moment, giving Isabel the chance to object, but the heap remained silent.

The little Muspratt sounded very much in command. 'I'm *so* glad,' she said. 'About eight?'

There was nothing to add, so Rebecca was about to ring off when she heard a further chirruping on the line. 'What?' she asked. 'Sorry, I didn't hear.'

'I said how's your daughter? Much happier, I'm sure, now she's home.'

Rebecca felt very tired. Isabel was involving her in too much nonsense. The mechanism was rusty, the joints creaked, the soldering was falling apart. God knew what might happen to her if this went on. 'Yes,' she said, but couldn't bring herself to add 'Much happier' as she had gloomily intended.

'We're up to our eyes in house decoration at the moment,' Phyllis said happily. 'I hope you won't mind . . .'

Happier? House decoration? Mind? Rebecca was bewildered. What was she doing, wasting valuable time? But the little Muspratt hadn't finished yet, oh no.

'Your roses must be looking lovely just now. I glimpse them from the lane when I'm passing.'

Glimpse. Of course. What do Muspratts do, Mummy? They glimpse, dear.

'Yes,' she said desperately. 'They're at their best now.'

'I'd love to come and see them some time. Well . . . Saturday, then?'

'Right,' Rebecca said, slamming the receiver down as though it were an iron.

14

Michael had thrown a bulging brief-case into the car so that he would have the excuse of work if too much entertainment threatened; but he intended to please his mother as far as possible and didn't bring it into the house with him. Phyllis intended to please her son as far as possible, and asked – sounding disappointed – whether he hadn't brought his work with him, she had put a table and a comfortable chair at the bottom of the garden so that he wouldn't be disturbed. They started, therefore, on the wrong foot, Michael feeling guilty at the furniture moving, Phyllis put out because he obviously wasn't going to treat her cottage as his home.

At least she had the sensitivity not to seat him at the head of the table. Remembering the look of misery and rage with which he had moved his place-mat on the night after Gerald died, she was prepared to go to great lengths to treat him as a small boy, or at least a boy home from school for a weekend of cake and mooching. He waited to be asked his opinion; she refrained from asking his opinion. He waited to have some responsible status forced on him; she prattled on about Fred, the handyman, and how well she was managing. He had vaguely dreaded having to support or even console her; she was bright as a cricket and, in her own words, happy as a lark. Having girded himself up for the visit, he felt at a loss. She hummed round the garden like a bee while he sprawled in the shade, frowning at a manuscript he wasn't reading. He even found himself wondering why on earth she had been so eager for him to come. His presence appeared to make very little difference.

Phyllis actually glowed with contentment as she glanced at the long, ramshackle figure in her garden chair. As always, her love went out to him with invisible arms, invisible bindings to cradle and wrap; while cutting flowers a hundred yards away, she hovered over him, ready to supply him with small comforts and protect him from the gnats. It was an easier, altogether softer feeling than loving Gerald had been. She had sometimes been quite annoyed with Gerald (suddenly, in the last week or so, she could admit such things); sometimes, particularly in the early years, Gerald had quite ... well, offended her, in the same sort of way that Fred had offended her the other evening. Michael never offended her. He was in many ways a mystery – though how someone who had been a feeding baby could turn out a mystery was a mystery in itself – but her respect for him was invincible; her love, although it contained plenty of sadness and disappointment, uncritical. To have him here, under her eye, was the most wonderful of pleasures. I mustn't disturb him. He'll see how I leave him alone. He likes that. She danced from flower to flower, smiling under her shady hat.

Michael, in fact, grew bored. When he was alone too long, particularly without music, his sense of identity – or lack of it – became uneasy. He needed to feel attached to something before he could have the illusion of being detached. In this unfamiliar, if pretty enough place, without his friends or his records, with very few reminders of his father – and certainly his mother wasn't one of them – all manner of vague doubts drifted into his mind. Thank God, he thought wryly, for Rebecca Broune and her barmy daughter.

They got through tea – tomato sandwiches and Simnel cake – and he offered to wash up but she wouldn't hear of it. What about letting him cook the dinner? Good gracious no, what an idea! There were very few books, and none of any interest. He searched the radio for music. 'Isn't it almost time for Desert Island Discs?' his mother asked, aproned over the sink. 'They have some good music on that sometimes.'

He went out and wandered down the field to the stream, she watching him through the window, flushed with delight. He leant on the gate and tried to take an intelligent interest in the cows, but his interest was not engaged. Slouching back up the hill, he wished he had a catapult or a cricket bat and a friendly child to play with. He found an old copy of the *New Statesman* in his brief-case and read that.

At least Phyllis let him see to the drinks and the wine. The weather was still unusually hot, the evening bringing no breeze, the shadows no relief. She had arranged things on the cobbles outside the back door, just so, a deck chair for everyone, two garden candles ready to light on the low wall. He hoped, half ironically and half protectively, that Rebecca Broune would appreciate these preparations.

Within three minutes of their arrival, he realized that Rebecca Broune appreciated very little. Wearing shapeless corduroys and a man's shirt, looking like an unrestored ruin and extremely nervous, she collapsed into a chair, lit a cigarette and inspected, through her dark glasses, the darkening horizon. Her daughter, a pale, plain woman, folded herself into the opposite chair and sat still. Phyllis, wearing what she had told him was just a simple frock – asking his opinion of it? he couldn't be sure – was very animated. Rebecca, abruptly cutting across the chatter, stated, 'I wasn't told you would be here.'

'Perhaps my mother thought you wouldn't come,' he said smoothly.

'Maybe she did. I might not have done.'

'Then I'm glad she kept quiet about it.'

She gave a suspicious grunt, and told Phyllis that she was going to look at the garden. 'I'm *ashamed* ...' Phyllis wailed, reluctantly following her.

'What do you do with yourself here?' he asked Isabel.

She shot him a wary glance. 'Nothing much.'

'Did you come from London?'

'No. I was in hospital.'

'I know,' he said patiently. 'I mean before that.'

'I lived in London.'

'What did you do?'

'Do?'

'Did you work?'

'I didn't do anything.' A long pause, a quick look towards the garden. 'I lived with someone.'

'A friend?'

'No. A man.'

'Not a friend.'

She puzzled for a moment, then flinched away. 'I told you.'

He was relieved to hear Phyllis and Rebecca coming back. '... and even if I could find anyone,' Phyllis was saying, 'Fred says it's best to wait and see what's here before deciding anything.' To Michael, it sounded as though she were talking about her husband.

'Ah. Fred. Well.' Rebecca sat down heavily. 'Fred knows, I'm sure.'

'He's going to cut everything back, he says, and dig over the beds in the autumn.'

'In the autumn,' Rebecca repeated. 'Is he now. Good for Fred.'

'I've been meaning to ask you – has Fred worked for you at all? I know you told me, but ...'

Michael noticed Rebecca hesitate. He felt it was not like Rebecca to hesitate. It was difficult to see her expression behind the sunglasses and the cigarette. He found himself hoping, unreasonably, that she would be kind.

'Yes,' she said casually, laying a long turd of ash in the ashtray. 'Fred did a bit of work for me once. Didn't he tell you? Years ago, though.' She smiled, though whether fondly or ironically it was impossible to tell. 'Interesting fellow. I'm glad you get on.'

That, thank God, seemed to be enough of Fred. Phyllis shepherded them indoors for dinner, because of the midges. She had placed Rebecca at the head of the table, herself at the foot, Michael and Isabel on either side. Within a few minutes, rather to Phyllis's surprise, Michael and Rebecca were deep in conversation – just what she had intended, of course, but it did leave her to take on Isabel alone, which wasn't easy.

'Your mother's a great gardener, isn't she. I do envy that sort of dedication.'

'Do you?' the girl asked. 'Why?'

'Well . . . it's so nice to have a hobby. Such an occupation. I know my husband would have been quite lost without his garden.'

'I think it's rather unhealthy, myself.'

'Unhealthy?' Phyllis was horrified. 'What an extraordinary thing to say! I would have thought gardening was one of the – well, healthiest things anyone could do. Fresh air, exercise . . .'

'That's not what I meant,' Isabel mumbled.

'Then' – kindly – 'what do you mean?'

'Nothing.'

She helped clear the plates. That was a good sign.

'It's a lovely dinner,' she said.

'Oh. Thank you. I'm so glad you like it.' Phyllis thought the girl might be quite normal if she were treated properly, washed her hair, wore a pretty dress. 'Do you enjoy cooking?'

'Yes.' Another long, difficult pause. 'Yes. I do.'

'You cook for your mother, I expect.'

'No. I don't.'

'Well – I'm sure she would appreciate it.'

'No. She wouldn't.'

In the silences of which Isabel's conversation seemed to be largely composed, Phyllis tried to get the drift of what Michael and Rebecca were talking about.

'Why should I?' Rebecca demanded belligerently.

'I can't answer that,' Michael said.

'Then how am I supposed to?'

'All right. You say you don't read, either. Why?'

Rebecca lit a cigarette and pushed her chair back from the table, making herself comfortable.

'Well. It seems irrelevant.'

'Irrelevant to what?'

'My life. Myself.'

'That's extraordinarily arrogant. If one only read what was relevant to oneself –'

'Yes, yes. I know that. I haven't the patience for their . . . trivial concerns. It's necessary to identify up to a point, isn't it?'

'What trivial concerns?'

'Sex. Dying. Little outrages.'

'Hardy concerned with little outrages? Proust?'

Rebecca snorted, pulling her chair round, humping over the table. 'Oh, my God. Literary talk.'

'A discussion about what you read is bound to be literary talk.'

'I thought you wanted to know why I *don't* read. And I told you.'

'But you implied a strong criticism of other writers – "trivial concerns"?'

'Then I should have said "in my opinion". Are you always so pedantic?'

Rebecca glared at Michael. He laughed. He liked her. Her face broke up gradually into various smiles, one following the other, increasing in confidence.

'You simply put the plums in a low oven,' Phyllis said, 'with some red wine and lemon peel – a *very* little sugar –'

'But what about the meringue?'

'Ah – the meringue. That takes a bit of care . . .'

She was aware that Rebecca occasionally glanced down the table to see how she was getting on with Isabel, but neither Rebecca nor Michael made any effort to include them in their conversation. She was a little ruffled by Michael's exclusive attention to Rebecca. It had been the point of the dinner party, but she hadn't expected it to turn out quite like this. Her remarks to Isabel became slightly malicious.

'It can't be altogether easy having a famous writer for a mother. I'm afraid Michael finds me very dull, but there it is – he gets enough intelligent conversation from his friends, I'm sure.'

'Isn't he married?'

'No. A confirmed bachelor.' She smiled forgivingly in Michael's direction. 'I don't know why that is, but I suppose it does happen.'

'Is he gay?'

'Gay? Oh, I see what you mean.' She was shocked, but mustn't show it. 'No, no. He has plenty of girl-friends.' Presumably he must have one or two. She really knew nothing about it. 'It's just that – well, I suppose he's not ready to settle down.'

'I never knew anybody who settled down.' It was hard to hear what the girl said, she mumbled so.

'Didn't you?' Phyllis looked coldly down the table at Rebecca and away again. 'No. I suppose you wouldn't.' The poor child. She hoped Rebecca had noticed the way she patted the girl's bony shoulder, her motherly concern. 'I promise you that most people are thoroughly settled. You will be too, one day.'

'I don't. I don't think so.'

'Of course you will. Why don't we go sight-seeing together some time? There are lots of interesting places – it's not much fun on one's own, is it? We could take a picnic ...' She went on inventing delights, quite carried away with the idea herself. Isabel looked younger and less dismal every minute. This part of the evening, anyway, was a success.

At eleven o'clock, and not a minute too soon, Rebecca decided to leave. She stood up, stubbed out her cigarette in the overflowing ashtray, and said, 'Well. We're off.' Isabel, who had been in the middle of one of Phyllis's sentences, looked grey again, the slight colour drained from her face without warning. She got up clumsily, muttering something about the dishes. 'That's all right,' Phyllis said, slipping her arm through Michael's. 'I've got a very good butler here.'

'Come and see the roses whenever you like.' Rebecca looked scathingly at her pinioned publisher. 'You'll be down again, I'm sure.'

'I'm sure I will.'

'Good. Come and see me. I hate people who just drop in, but it's no use phoning.'

'And we must meet,' Phyllis said to Isabel, meaning it. 'Just call in any time. You could practise your cooking, that'd be fun.'

Isabel nodded emphatically. Rebecca's eyebrows shot up, as though in cruel comment that wonders would never cease. She made a clumsy herding gesture. 'Come along, then. We can't have you out at all hours.' It was, even Phyllis realized, a mockery of what she herself might have said. They walked down the path in silence, Isabel diminished, almost obliterated in her mother's rakish shadow.

'Well!' Phyllis said. 'There you are!' She would like to have sat down with Michael for a while, had a real post-mortem, but automatically started clearing the table.

'Don't do that,' he said. 'I'll do it when you've gone to bed.'

She didn't know whether it was a genuine offer of help or whether he just wanted to get rid of her. Uncertainty, hesitation, hope, passed through her eyes in a cloud. She dithered, holding two vegetable dishes.

'Are you quite sure?'

'Certain. What about a brandy?'

She put the dishes down in an instant. This was more like it. They sat over the debris almost as comfortably as though she had been with Fred.

'She's an interesting woman,' Michael said thoughtfully. 'I'm glad I met her.'

'Good.' Phyllis felt very proud. 'It can't be much fun being her daughter, though.'

'Well. I'm not. Thank God.'

'No, but Isabel is.' She felt very worldly again, almost his equal. 'She's not nearly such a little mouse as she seems. Quite opinionated, in fact.'

'Mm . . .' He wasn't thinking about Isabel. 'I wonder what she writes in those notebooks of hers.'

'What notebooks?'

'She says she keeps notebooks.'

'Well, darling. Since you get on so famously, why don't you ask her?'

He woke up, recognized her, smiled. 'Yes,' he said. 'I will.'

Phyllis missed Michael after he left on Sunday afternoon, but not acutely. She believed he would come back soon, and if it would be to see Rebecca Broune rather than herself, well, you couldn't blame him, writers were his job after all. In the meanwhile, she had scored a small triumph with Isabel, and there was Fred to think about. Well, of course, not Fred to think about, but things that Fred might do to think about. He had finished the bathroom, all but the gloss paint – it had looked very nice over the weekend, with the new curtains and the pine toilet seat (Fred had a way of finding everything) and a new bathmat from the Co-Op which would do until she could get a better one in London. Now, perhaps, he could see to the sockets and the draughts. There must come a time, she supposed, when there would be nothing left for Fred to do. She wouldn't think about it. What she had said about the digging in the autumn hadn't been strictly true; that is, she hadn't actually suggested it to Fred yet. She was sure he would agree. 'Certainly, Mrs M. Yours to command.'

When he arrived on Monday he seemed just a little off-colour. He asked whether the bed had held up, but painted without his usual humming and whistling.

'This heat's getting me down,' he said. 'That office is like an oven.'

'Would you like a cold drink? A nice long lemonade with ice?'

'No, thanks, Mrs M.' But in a few minutes he called out, 'I wouldn't mind a nice long Scotch, if you've got one.'

She was sitting outside the back door doing some mending – never leave a button or a loose hem, if you do it'll never get done – when he came out and flopped down beside her, just as he was in his overalls. 'Flaked out,' he said. 'Dizzy. Smell of paint, I suppose.'

She was immediately concerned, offering him aspirin, suggesting he lay down for a little while. He looked at her quizzically and put his hand over hers. Appalled, fascinated, she watched her hand disappear, felt the heat of his, heavy on top of it. She sat there trapped, very uncomfortable, but longing not to offend him.

'You're a funny little lady,' he said. 'Sometimes I don't know what you're at.'

'At?' She giggled nervously. 'I'm not at anything. Except' – pointedly – 'my mending.'

'How old are you, anyway? Fifty-five? Sixty?'

This was too much. She took her hand away – dragged it, really, since his was so passive – and said clumsily, 'That's no business whatever of yours.'

'Ah,' he said, smiling. 'Sixty. Maybe more?'

'You're most impertinent, Mr Skerry!' She jumped up, kicking over her work-basket, cotton reels rolled in all directions, pins slid out of their box and into the cracks between the bricks. 'Oh!' she screamed softly. 'Now look what you've made me do!'

He was howling with laughter. She couldn't remember seeing a man laugh so hard. With tears in his eyes, gasping, he managed to say, 'Calm down, Mrs M., calm down,' then rocked again, mopping his eyes with a rather dirty handkerchief.

'I know you enjoy a joke,' she said, prim but wavering. 'I don't find crass bad manners at all humorous, unfortunately.'

'Bad manners!' He was off again. 'You're a wonder, Mrs M.! Bad manners!'

'Mrs Broune told me we wouldn't get on,' she said, extremely dignified. 'I couldn't understand what she meant until now. If asking impertinent questions and behaving in a – familiar way is your idea of a joke, I doubt whether you "get on" with any of your employers.'

He sobered, but slowly. She noticed one of his eyes had begun to twitch, which she knew to be a sign of tension. 'Mrs

Broune,' he said. 'Ah. Mrs Broune.' He seemed to be sizing her up, his gaze, except for the twitching eye, straight and friendly. 'Well,' he said. 'You know Mrs Broune . . .'

She felt at a disadvantage and began fussily picking up the cotton reels.

'I thought we were getting on very well,' he said quietly. 'You wouldn't take her word against me, would you? As for the indiscretion – I told you, Phil, all's fair in love and war. Sorry if I upset you, though.'

Now she wanted to cry. It wasn't fair. It wasn't right of him to spoil everything. She went and stood by the little wall with her back to him, biting her lips and blinking. He came up behind her and said, very humbly, 'Sorry, Mrs M.' and when she gave him a cold look he held out his hand, frank as the first day, and asked, 'Friends?' After a moment's hesitation, she took it. His grip was firm and business-like. She said, 'Very well. But please think before you speak in future.'

'Yes, mam. Certainly, mam.' His salute was as cocky as ever. 'Now then. Let's get that bathroom polished off, shall we?'

He didn't stay for his nightcap and, far worse, he said he wouldn't be able to come the following evening. 'One of my ladies is in trouble – something wrong with her boiler, if you'll pardon the expression. Sorry, Mrs M., I know you don't like that kind of joke, very poor taste. But you mustn't think you're the only pebble on the beach, you know. Poor old Fred is a knight-errant. Well, errant anyway.'

'But I did hope to get the sockets done this week,' she said querulously.

'So you shall. No problem. I'll see you on Wednesday.' He patted her cheek in a friendly way. 'Keep smiling.' For the first time, he bundled his good clothes under his arm and went off in his overalls. Even his car sounded relieved.

What could she do about Fred? He was getting tired of her. She faced the fact that she didn't care tuppence about the wretched sockets or the draughts. She wanted his cheery whistle, his 'Ta-ra! Ta-ra!', his competence, the way he sat quietly in the evenings, enjoying himself. She was horrified. Sitting alone with her brandy – a glass didn't seem to last as long as it did two weeks ago – she wondered if she could possibly be, no of course she couldn't, and yet if she was, and yet how *could* she be. No, she just liked Fred, that's all. Liked him very much. Gerald would have liked him too, she was sure. He had never given her a bill. Perhaps – could it be? – that was the trouble. Perhaps he wanted some money, and quite right too. Paying him would put everything right, get them back on a proper footing. That was the first thing she would ask him on Wednesday – 'How much do I owe you, Fred?'

But he didn't come on Wednesday. Instead, there was a formal telephone call. 'I'm phoning from the office, Mrs Muspratt. I'm afraid I shan't be able to make it this evening. Would Friday be convenient?'

Friday? It was aeons away. It was the end of the week. 'But Fred – you promised!'

'I don't like to disappoint you, but something's come up. Shall we say Friday?'

'All right, but Fred, how much –' He had rung off.

She drank rather too much brandy that evening and the result, the mumbling stumble up the stairs, the clothes dropped anyhow, the awful nausea, shocked her. She refused to go to pieces because of a handyman. It was unseemly, unreasonable and downright wrong. If only she had some responsibility, some call on her time. She rang Rebecca Broune's number. Isabel, sounding much further away than the end of the road, answered. 'I wondered if you'd like a little trip,' Phyllis said. 'I'm tired of sitting about in this heat. We could go wherever you like – to the Abbey, perhaps.'

'Yes,' Isabel said.

'I'll pick you up, then. If you stand by the gate you'll see me coming. In about twenty minutes?'

'Yes,' Isabel said.

Phyllis behaved very merrily on the way. She opened the sunshine roof – a great extravagance and she hadn't thought she'd ever use it honestly – and they bowled along the lanes at a spanking pace, two women out on a spree.

'One gets a little morbid sometimes,' Phyllis said, sitting erect with bright eyes on the road. 'Everyone does. There's nothing like a day out in lovely weather to blow the cobwebs away.'

'I shouldn't think you were ever morbid,' Isabel muttered.

'Oh, you'd be surprised. There are lots of bogies about, even for old women like me.'

'You're not old.' A long pause and then, as Phyllis glanced at her, the girl smiled, showing small, pointed teeth. 'I think you're very pretty.'

'Be that as it may,' Phyllis said, enormously pleased, 'I have my gloomy moments, I promise you.'

When they reached the old wool town she was conscious for the first time that she was driving towards Bamfield. It was as though a new Phyllis Muspratt were trying to take charge of her, tempting her with brandy, leading her off in search of Fred.

'What would you like to do? There wasn't time to make a picnic so I thought we'd stop for lunch somewhere. There's a National Trust castle round here, I think – or would you like to go on and see the Abbey?'

'The Abbey,' Isabel said. Then, after a mile of silence, 'I like churches. I believe in them.'

'Do you really?' It was commendable, of course, but a little strange. What a funny girl, impossible to realize she was almost Sophia's age. 'Why is that?'

'I don't know.' Phyllis glanced at her again. The wind from the open roof had blown her hair about. She really didn't have an unattractive little face – eyes too small, nose too sharp, unhealthy skin – but basically it wasn't at all bad. 'I'd like to be a nun,' Isabel said.

'Oh, I don't think you want to be a nun. Think of all the fun you'd miss.'

Isabel didn't answer that, and Phyllis herself thought it a foolish remark. A nun, after all, must lead a settled life. 'Are you hungry?' she asked.

'No.'

'Then we'll have lunch after. What a beautiful day. What a charming town this is.' And so on, pointing things out, congratulating them for being quaint, spreading her blessing. She parked the car neatly in the proper place, shut the roof, locked it, made sure the doors were fast. Then, with a brisk step and the expression of a woman arriving on time for an entertainment she was determined to enjoy, Phyllis challenged the Abbey.

'I'm not very good at churches myself,' she chattered, as they passed through shadows of ancient yew and cypress. 'It's so much nicer outside. Still, it's always fascinating to see history. One wonders' – tilting her head to look up and up at the great arch of the western front – 'how in the world they *did* it.'

Isabel was silent. Once the swing doors had closed silently behind them, she wandered off on her own. There were a few tourists walking about quietly, and a couple of busy vergers bustling round like housewives, but the immense nave was undisturbed, the mid-day silent. Phyllis avoided walking on the brasses. She paused with moderate wonder at ancient tombs. The place seemed dedicated to death, chapels and sepulchres, sarcophagi and cenotaphs; a real mausoleum, though it had nothing to do with death as Phyllis understood it, there was nothing bright or hopeful, no ray of sunshine. Her arms were chilly under the thin sleeves. She wondered what Fred would think of it, or whether in fact he had ever been there, summing up the condition of the stone and the likelihood of the stained glass lasting a few more hundred years. She found Isabel standing by a monument.

'Who's that?' Phyllis asked, unable to read the inscription without her glasses.

'Somebody called John Wakeman. He was the last Abbot.'

There was an unusual note in Isabel's voice: life. 'Isn't it wonderful?'

'Is it?' Phyllis peered uncertainly. The recumbent stone skeleton didn't look very wonderful to her. It looked morbid.

'Look. It's decayed, you see. There's a mouse gnawing his stomach – and a snake in his shroud, here – and a worm on his knee. There's a snail crawling up his left arm and look, here's a frog. It's wonderful.'

'My dear girl! It's revolting! What a horrible idea!' Phyllis felt thoroughly upset. How was one supposed to look on the bright side, let alone believe in the resurrection of the body (which of course she didn't, but it was a comforting idea), with such unnecessary reminders of mortality? She wanted to hurry Isabel away, but the girl seemed transfixed. She traced the stone folds of the shroud with a thin finger, touched the eye sockets, lingered over the dreadful, almost indistinguishable mouse. It was as though some inner light had suddenly been switched on. She was like a woman at prayer, breathless with revelation. She couldn't bear to leave it, and when Phyllis finally got her away, almost marching her up the aisle, she ran back for a last look. Phyllis, disapproving, waited in the good warm sunshine.

'They didn't have a postcard,' Isabel said.

'Perhaps they don't think it's one of their more attractive monuments,' Phyllis snapped. 'I really think I'm going to have a gin and tonic. I feel quite chilly.'

Still, there was no doubt that the unhappy Abbot had made a great change in Isabel. She was really quite good company. She almost chattered. Phyllis bought her a pair of pretty sandals, the kind she wore herself, with a small heel, so much nicer than those dilapidated things the girl was wearing even if they did come from Delos as she said. They browsed in a bookshop – Phyllis bought a charming book on birds for Jasper – and looked at a very dull museum. Then they had tea, expensive, but at least the scones were homemade, and set off for home.

The nearer they got, the more their roles were reversed. Phyllis, thinking of the empty evening, the almost empty brandy decanter, the wretched absence of Fred, became silent. Isabel, still fired with this peculiar energy, prattled on in short, breathless sentences. She had lived with a Greek who had beaten her up. Well, he couldn't help it. He was a very mixed-up man, that was why she had lived with him. She thought he'd get on better without her. She seemed to infuriate him somehow. He wouldn't leave her, though. She didn't think she could have borne it if he had. So the only solution had seemed to get rid of herself. That hadn't worked either, but at least he had gone back to Greece, so maybe he was happier.

'It seems to me,' Phyllis said, 'that it's your own happiness you should be thinking about. He sounds most unpleasant.' It was odd how people like Rebecca Broune seemed to infect the world around them. She had no doubt that Rebecca was responsible for this squalid way of life. Isabel had no example, no proper standards of behaviour. A week ago she would have said all this, or most of it, but somehow she didn't feel so sure of her ground; questions about herself, about her own life, kept popping up in the most disturbing way.

'You need a home of your own,' she said, thinking of Sophia and feeling a sudden longing for her grandchildren. 'That would give you an anchor.'

'But to be anchored you have to have shallow water, don't you?'

'Not necessarily,' Phyllis said. 'Ships anchor in very stormy seas, I believe.'

They passed the Brigadier's shanty town, reeking in the heat, no one about.

'What is that horrible place?'

'It's where the Brigadier's workmen live – and their families, I suppose.'

'Those men. I've seen them in the village. Mother calls them the Brig Boys.'

'Yes.' Phyllis realized that she had almost forgotten about the Brig Boys. She saw them, of course, in the lane, and swarming along the road to Lamberts Heath on their motor bikes. She heard them at nights sometimes, screaming up the hill with their terrible music. But since she had a man about the place, she hadn't been frightened of them. He must stay, she thought desperately; he's got to stay.

'I am sick when I see them,' Isabel mumbled.

Of course. She's alone, poor girl. Phyllis drove her home and waited until she was through the gate, protected. She was unrecognizable from the dour, dim little creature who had climbed into the car this morning.

'It was a lovely day,' Isabel called out. 'I'm glad we went to the Abbey.'

'Yes. Well, don't brood about that horrible tomb. Or those silly boys. Come and see me soon.'

'I will. Thanks for the sandals.' She raised her voice, spelling it out as though Phyllis were deaf. 'I LIKE BEING WITH YOU.'

Phyllis waved through the roof as she drove off. Now, her heart sunk so low, she wished she had asked the girl to stay for supper. It would have been easier to avoid the brandy decanter, the only consoling thing waiting for her in the empty house. Oh, Fred, please come back. She firmly put the decanter, the sherry and Fred's whisky back in the cupboard and made herself eat a poached egg, though she didn't want it. She telephoned Sophia, but only got the baby-sitter. Bron was away for the night, the baby-sitter said, and Sophia had gone out somewhere. Strange. Sophia never went out by herself. There was so much about life that she didn't know. So much, after all, that she didn't know how to deal with. She felt old, very ignorant.

Thursday passed in the same, unrelenting glare of heat. She made herself unpack the toys she had brought from Surrey, in case Jasper came to stay soon. She liked arranging them in the attic, though it was intolerably hot up there. Jasper and

Selina seemed to promise a kind of return to innocence. She could rest in their company, somehow – what a curious thought – be her proper age. She tried Sophia again, but there was no reply.

On Friday afternoon she was very nervous. She must pull herself together before he came. She must ask how much she owed him. She must be friendly but distant, appealing but firm. The air was growing thicker, hotter; she could hardly breathe. The prospect of thunder alarmed her and she hoped Fred would arrive before it started. She hoped, on the other hand, that he might telephone and say he wasn't coming. She hurried about and kept pausing, wondering what she was hurrying for. What should she wear? No, she mustn't change her dress, she mustn't put on those unsuitable slacks again. She compromised by quickly combing her hair, dabbing a little cologne on her temples and behind her ears. The last hour seemed interminable. When she heard his car draw up, on the dot of seven, it was as though she had been injected with a great feeling of calm, a reassurance that God was in his heaven and all right with her world.

16

Fred was a little drunk. He made no bones about it – 'Just a little tiddly, Mrs M., to tell you the truth. It's my birthday.'

'Well!' she said. 'Many happy returns.' She wasn't prepared for it, though. The whisky on his breath, his unusually bright eyes and flushed face, disconcerted her terribly. 'Before we talk about sockets, could you let me know how much I owe you?'

'Owe me?' He dropped his overalls and old shirt on the toilet seat, but they fell on the floor. He propped himself in the bathroom doorway. 'You mustn't talk like that, Mrs M. I told you – I don't do it for the money, I'm not a money-minded man.'

'Nevertheless,' she said sharply, 'I should like a bill.'

'Oh, you would, would you?' He lurched slightly, his shoulder slipping off the lintel. 'Well, we'll have to see what we can do.' He didn't close the door completely and she heard him stumbling about, swearing softly to himself. It was getting very dark. There was an ominous rumbling of thunder. She sat down in the wingchair and pretended to be reading Henry James.

'All right,' he said behind her. 'What about these sockets, then?'

She turned and saw a weird white shape in the doorway. Except for his patterned underpants, he was completely naked. He took a deep breath, drawing in his stomach muscles. 'Stripped for action, you see. Fine figure of a man, eh Phil?'

She wanted to tell him to put his clothes on immediately, but she was frightened. She dropped the book and picked it up quickly, not knowing where to look. His private parts – really, it was disgraceful, he should keep them private – bulged through the thin cotton. Apart from that, she could only see the white of him, his teeth, his glimmering stomach, his short, muscular legs. She must ignore his nakedness, try to take it as a matter of course. There was no question of going upstairs. She said, 'I need one on the side there. For the mixer.'

'For the mixer, eh?' He peered uncertainly at the wall. He couldn't see anything in the gloom. There was another eruption of thunder, closer this time. His pale back glistened with sweat. She could smell it.

'Perhaps you'd better put the light on,' she said stiffly.

'No need, no need.' The bread board fell with a loud slam on to the tiled floor, followed by the splintering crash of a jam jar. 'Now, Fred,' he admonished himself. 'Breaking up the happy home, that won't do.'

'Perhaps you'd better –' she began. She was going to say 'go home now', but suddenly the kitchen was bared in a white flash of lightning followed by a clap of thunder so loud, so immediately overhead, that she uttered a little cry of fear.

'Scared of thunder?' Fred asked. 'Poor Mrs M. Poor little Mrs M.' He was lumbering round the table towards her. Nothing would stop him. There was nowhere to run to, nowhere to hide. She got behind the chair but he pushed it away. Another flash of lightning showed his face beaming with bleary friendliness, Fred's own face, not a monster. When the thunder came he groped for her, caught her, lifted her against his hot, damp chest. She now knew he was laughing. 'It's all right, Phil. Fred's here.'

She struggled. Lifted from the floor, her legs kicked dizzily, like a clockwork toy, her fists pummeled. She was small and easily held, even in her frantic action. His voice was full of the fun of it. 'Quite a little wild-cat, aren't you? Come on now, Mrs M., where are your manners?'

'Put me down!' she screamed, though the sound came out thin. 'Let go of me!'

He lowered her quite gently to the floor. Her legs, trembling, at least supported her. She was panting, dishevelled with the exertion. Very deliberately, still vastly amused, he undid the top button of her dress. Then the next. She gawped at him in the thick light, the thin darkness. Her mouth hung open. She couldn't see anything. Her eyes had died. She made an inhuman noise, back in her throat. It was such a dreadful sound, so ugly and pitiful, that it brought her to her senses.

'What do you think you're doing?' she demanded. 'Leave me alone.'

He undid the third button. Still smiling. 'Take it off,' he said. 'I wish to see your body, Mrs M.'

With extraordinary agility she doubled herself up and ran beneath his arm like a crab. She reached the back door, struggled with the latch, flung it open on to the angry night. Another flare of lightning lit up the little yard, the four deckchairs, the two round candles on the wall. She stepped back involuntarily. He was leaning on the table, one white leg bent and crossed over the other in the stance of a Victorian gentleman in an oleograph. She knew, somehow, that his expression had changed, but with the resounding, reverberating explosion of thunder she couldn't hear what he said. It didn't matter anyway. She fumbled for the light switch. His nakedness sprang to life, the spilt jam, the broken glass, his bare feet crossed as though in velvet slippers. But she had never seen that face before. It was cold as stone, the colour of stone. It was sharp, with jagged edges.

'Then I can't help you, can I?'

The summer evenings, the companionship, the furtive nourishment taken by her heart, the jokes, the dreams of autumn and even winter, the sense of being cared for, her own silly laughter. She was attacked by mourning. For one insane moment – the only insane moment in her life so far – she wanted to run to him, bury her head, let him do what he liked. But she waited, her hand on the door latch, trying to control her trembling.

He shrugged his shoulders and went into the bathroom. She stayed by the open door. The thunder had prowled away, was snarling over the distant hills. It started to rain, a vertical downpour that flooded the cobbles in a moment, splashing on to the kitchen floor. He came back, neat as ever, knotting his tie, his overalls in a bundle under his arm, his tools in a canvas bag.

'You can post me the bill,' she said in a high, certain voice.

'No problem.' He put the bag and the overalls down, took a piece of paper from his inside pocket and threw it on the table. 'I'm always prepared for eventualities, Mrs M. You can post me a cheque.'

He went out into the rain, swinging down the front path, looking up and about at the rain as though it were a good thing, good for the garden. His car door slammed, the engine started. She realized that she was holding on to the latch as though her arm were a tether. The sound of the car roared up the hill, faded, was gone.

With a little whimper, she let go of the latch and sat down. 'Oh dear,' she said aloud. 'Oh dear, oh dear.' After a few minutes she got up and went to the cupboard, poured herself a brandy with shaking hands, drained the glass standing up, poured another, coaxing the last drop out of the empty decanter. 'Oh dear,' she kept saying. 'Oh ...' She wandered across the kitchen, noticed the broken glass, wandered back again. She was trembling as though she had an ague. Who could she ask for help? Why did she need help? It was all over. But suppose he came back? She was sure he would come back. He knew where she kept the spare key, on a flowerpot behind the hedge. She was so forgetful, she was afraid of locking herself out. She must move the key. But it was raining so hard. 'Oh my God, oh my goodness ...' Should she telephone Rebecca Broune? What would she say? It would sound ridiculous. It would merely humiliate her more. An old woman subjected to this, to this. She didn't know what to call it. Horror. Insult. Outrage. And yet she wasn't angry. She was just sickened, shocked, desolate. She sat unconsciously rocking herself, moaning a little, hunched over her empty glass. After a while she went to the cupboard again and half-filled the glass with whisky, then sat like a small, frightened animal, the rain splashing unheeded through the open door.

She didn't know how or when she got to bed. Sometime during the night she realized that she hadn't undressed and made feeble movements before falling unconscious again. She heard someone blundering along the lane – coming into her garden? – and sat up, half off the bed, every sense strained through the fog and ache of the whisky; then fell back again, snoring with little clicks. It was ten o'clock before she finally woke up and lay wretchedly staring at the pink silk hill of her eiderdown, thrown off during the night. She felt wrecked, anchorless. The sensible voice that told her nothing had happened, she hadn't been raped, it had just been a very unpleasant incident, was very far away. It was growing fainter. It had almost gone. What was she going to do? How could she go on without Fred, without Gerald, without Fred, for ever?

At last she pulled off her clothes, put on her dressing gown, stumbled down the stairs, struggling as usual to open the wretched door. What had Fred said it needed? She shuffled across the kitchen, avoiding the broken glass, put the kettle on. It was a wet, chilly morning. There was a bill and a circular on the floor under the letter box. She picked them up, bending with difficulty, and put them on the table. She saw the piece of paper Fred had left, but didn't know where she had put her glasses. She had no eyes, no strength, no common sense; she hardly seemed to remember how to make tea, puzzling over the heaped teaspoon, her hand still shaking as she poured on the boiling water. Tears began pouring out of her eyes in little spurts. She sat at the table crying, huddled in her dressing gown, sipping the scalding tea.

When she heard a car stop she stiffened, sick with fear, staring at the front door as though it might open of its own accord. The gate clicked. Footsteps up the path. The rat-tat of the knocker, not very peremptory, rather timid. He had come to apologize. It was a remorseful knock. Shamefaced, even bashful, standing on the doorstep with his grin suitably sobered, holding out his hand, 'Friends, Mrs M.?' She gathered her dressing gown together, tried ineffectually to smooth her tangled hair. 'You must understand, Fred, the very next time you ...'

But it was Sophia. Alone. 'Hi, Mother,' she said, and walked in.

The impossible had happened. Sophia and Bron had talked about his affair. About all his affairs. She had left him. Walked out on Selina and Jasper. That was it. That was the end.

The idea of going to her mother didn't occur to her until she was almost out of London. She drove expertly, fast, with care. She sat very straight, manipulating the gears, adjusting the rear mirror, her small face the colour and substance of old marble, her eyes watchful. Anger possessed her. It had come, she thought, from nowhere. Wham, bang, and there was anger. If she hadn't left she might have murdered him. Murdered someone. She had gone straight past Selina playing on the floor, Jasper drawing at the kitchen table. It was Saturday. He had the weekend to think of what to do. She, Sophia, was out of it.

But she had to go somewhere. Her mother's was the obvious place. Her mother's life was an empty room waiting for occupation. Her mother's routine, her placid acceptance of rain or shine, her unshakeable benevolence, were just what Sophia needed. Appalling grief and guilt at leaving Selina would certainly attack her sooner or later. Her mother would manage it, make it appear bearable, shape it as she shaped her pastry, disposing of ragged edges, her uncontrollable feelings would be ordered, given names and practical solutions. In the ordinary course of events, she thought her mother trivial and unduly possessive. These were just the qualities she wanted just now. Cryck was a wonderful, a miraculous convenience.

So she said, 'Hi, Mother,' and when Phyllis started jumping up and down, exclaiming, fussing, Sophia sat down wrapped in her tragedy, not noticing the jam and the broken glass, her mother's dishevelled appearance, the stale smell, the unwashed glass.

'What's happened?' Phyllis demanded. 'Where are the children? Where's Bron?'

'I've left him,' Sophia said, and began to cry.

'Oh, my dear. Oh, darling. I'll make some more tea.'

This was exactly right. Sophia sobbed. Phyllis made the tea, darting across now and then to hug Sophia, to pat her, hurrying back again to wash out the teapot, warm it, keeping up a constant tut-tut, apparently perfectly normal. But her heart, that suddenly unwieldy organ, sank with terrible dismay, over-burdened. I can't cope with this. I can't deal with it. I can't — meaning her heart couldn't — rise to the occasion. She waited for Sophia to look at her; to notice the disarray in the kitchen. Sophia noticed nothing but her own broken life.

'I'll just put some clothes on,' Phyllis said, desperately wondering what to do first, deciding she could cope better if she were dressed at least. 'Will you be all right for a minute?'

Sophia nodded, tearing off four sheets from the roll of paper towels Phyllis had put at her elbow.

Phyllis was in a turmoil. Her whole instinct was to throw herself into Sophia's trouble, tackle it as best she could. Her instinct was still there, but it was powerless. It was she who needed Sophia's help. What a dreadful thing to think. It was she, a grandmother, who needed a mother; she who should be weeping into the paper towels, comforted with tea. Dear oh dear, what a muddle. How unnatural, how cruel. Maybe Sophia had been sent by God or Fate or something to bring her to her senses; but if so, God or Fate had been mistaken. She was inadequate. This was Rebecca's life, not Phyllis Muspratt's. She hurried downstairs almost hoping to find her darling daughter gone.

Sophia was sniffing and shuddering. It had been the bald statement 'I've left him' that had set her off, and she already felt a little better. Nevertheless, she was in unfamiliar country. The bleak place, desolate and cold as hell, hell itself, had been there all the time. She knew that. She had also known that it would only take one step in the wrong direction, just the slightest relaxing of vigilance, to land her there. It was her own fault. Not Bron's. She could bear being angry with Bron – that, literally, was child's play. But she couldn't bear being angry with herself. Her mother would take that over; even if her mother scolded her it would be a relief. On the other hand, if her mother said she must of course divorce Bron, no question, that would be a relief too. So she waited, recklessly ripping off paper towels, summoning her considerable forces of argument before deciding in which direction they should go.

'Well ...' Phyllis said. And then, cowardly, 'I'll just clear up this mess – so silly, I knocked the jam over –' She hid on her hands and knees with the dustpan and the scrubbing brush. When that was done, she had to sit down; she had to say, 'Tell me all about it.'

Sophia began hesitantly. She had never spoken about it before – until, that is, the terrible row with Bron this morning, after he had come home with those dreadful words 'Look, I think we should talk', and that had been very different; she hadn't spoken then, she had mumbled and screamed and finally, giving up words altogether, hit him. Then she had been sick, vomiting in the spotless basin, over her own hair. It didn't bear thinking about. So she mumbled now, but since it was her mother, a mere shadow, and not Bron, she quickly gained confidence and the words streamed out in perfect order.

Phyllis listened meekly. Sometimes, remembering, she interjected a tut-tut, a little groan of sympathy. Bron had been having these affairs, these things, for some time. Well, Sophia didn't blame him. It wasn't that. She knew she wasn't, well, perhaps she wasn't much fun in bed but she was so worried all the time, it was all right for men but of course she wouldn't take the pill – you didn't go out of your way to get cancer, did you? – and she hated the idea of having some foreign body inside her, she meant the coil of course, and she was terrified of getting pregnant again, terrified. So she knew that wasn't much help to Bron, but what could she do? She wouldn't dream of asking him to have a vasectomy, why should he, anyway he wouldn't do it, supposing she and the children got run over, it happened all the time.

No, what she couldn't stand, what really upset her, wasn't the actual *sex*, it was – well, she didn't know how to explain it – it was the *nice time* he had with these women, it was the fact that he talked to them and went to discos with them and took them to the movies, and they had no children to worry about, they could go out any time they liked, they could spend hours over their hair and their – well, it was all that. It was so bitterly unfair. She was just a drudge, a convenience. He had no respect for her. He thought he could divide his life up into nice neat little compartments, and hers was labelled Wife, skivvy. Didn't he think *she* would like to go out sometimes, talk about something other than Jasper and Selina, his boring office, dreary advertising? Not that she could, of course. It was she, not Bron, who had to do all the economizing, managing somehow on tuppence ha'penny. And she was so tired all the time. But she didn't see why this should make him risk every-thing – Jasper and Selina – (she began to cry again) – his whole *life* – just for nothing, just for enjoying himself.

Phyllis made a feeble movement towards her, but she was off again, she had changed gear. Well, she had put up with it so long as it didn't *interfere*. She had settled for it. That was the way things had to be, she had told herself, and so long as he kept quiet about it she could manage. But he had actually expected her to *discuss* the situation, as though it were, as though it were something *else* he expected her to deal with. Not just the children and the house and the meals and the money, but his beastly affairs as well. She might as well have them all to stay. Perhaps he'd like that. They could watch television while she cooked their supper. *After* getting the children into bed, mind you. Well, she couldn't put up with that. She might be stupid, but that – no, it was the end. If she didn't get out, she was done for.

'Well,' Phyllis said. 'Well ...' She was quite bewildered. 'What about the children?'

'They must manage somehow. Let him see what it's like not to be able to go out whenever he wants to. Let him see what it's like to have them round his feet all day, every day, half the night too sometimes.'

'But what about ... when he has to go to work?'

'Too bad. People manage. If I worked, I'd be expected to manage, wouldn't I?'

Sophia was frightening in her resolve: little Sophia, sweet, good, complicated Sophia, what had happened to her? And that nice Bron. And those lovely children. Oh dear, oh dear, I don't know what to think. But she couldn't say that. What was it she ought to say? I was assaulted last night – yes, assaulted, your own mother, Jasper's Granny. That wouldn't do. She was failing Sophia. How were they going to get through the day? How was she going to shop, cook, provide support? Where was Michael? Where was Gerald?

'Daddy would have been ... terribly upset,' she said helplessly.

'Yes. I expect he would. I'm sorry.'

'Oh, you mustn't be sorry. I'm glad you came. I'm really glad you came. It's not your fault, it's just that – well, it's rather a shock. I always thought you and Bron were so happy, so settled ...'

'We are. We were. But –'

'Then don't you think – I mean isn't it a little – rather a strong measure?'

'Probably. I had to do it, that's all.'

Well, then. Now what do we do? Get roaring drunk, Rebecca said. 'I'll have to do some shopping, I'm afraid. I'm terribly sorry, but –'

'Life must go on,' Sophia said with a despairing giggle. 'I know. Poor old Mum. It's really a bit much –', and she began to cry again.

They got through the morning, but Sophia never stopped

talking about it. Of course not. One couldn't expect her to. They went to Lamberts Heath in Sophia's Renault and loaded up with provisions. Sophia bought two very expensive toys for Jasper and Selina. Sometimes she seemed to forget that she wasn't going to see them again, then it would come over her and she looked sick, her eyes filled with tears. Phyllis was sure Fred's car would be parked outside when they got back. She was so anxious that she stopped listening, craning forward to look through the windscreen, ready with some explanation, though she didn't know what it would be. There was no car. They had a cold lunch, which Sophia didn't eat. Whenever she paused in her exposition, Phyllis tried to think of something to say that would throw new light on the situation. She tried desperately to think of a suggestion, a practical plan. But Sophia was inflexible. Having discovered hell, she was determined to stay there.

There was a cold drizzle, summer temporarily done for by the storm. They couldn't go outside. There was nothing to do but sit and talk, talk and sit. By three o'clock Phyllis's need for a change, an occupation, a drink, became unbearable. She smuggled the new bottle of brandy into the bathroom and drank some from a toothmug. Sophia kept watering the tea until it was quite colourless. Even when she took a short rest – 'Oh well. There it is,' and Phyllis daringly suggesting that worse things happened at sea – she didn't look round at the room, didn't ask questions, but told anecdotes about Selina and Jasper. It was not unlike the awful day when Gerald died, except that Sophia, not Phyllis, was in the widow's role. But there was no cremation or Will to discuss. It was just going over and over the same thing, amazing to Sophia, horribly remote to her mother. Time dragged; sometimes, to Phyllis, seemed to stop altogether. Then she would hurry off to the bathroom again, taking the brandy from under last night's underwear in the laundry tub, careful to flush the lavatory and run the tap.

The telephone rang at five. They looked at it, and at each

other. It was Fred, of course. She would be very cool and reasonable: 'Yes, Mr Skerry, I understand . . . Perhaps you had better come round and discuss the matter.' Though how could he, with Sophia there? On the other hand, how could she go out, meet him anywhere?

'I'd better answer it,' she said unsteadily. 'It's probably my handyman.' She stumbled over the flex, but Sophia didn't notice.

'Phyllis? Bron. Is Sophia there?'

She stared stupidly at the receiver.

'Bron?' Sophia whispered.

Phyllis nodded. She was dizzy.

'I'm sure she's there,' Bron said. 'Can I speak to her, please?'

Phyllis held out the receiver. Sophia shook her head violently. Phyllis said, 'You must.' She wondered if she was going to be sick. Sophia sighed, and took the receiver. She didn't say anything for a minute. Then, in a very odd voice, quite unlike her own, she said, 'Yes, Bron?'

Phyllis staggered to the bathroom and washed her face. I mustn't give up like this. I must manage, I must manage. She sat down on the lavatory and took some deep breaths. Sophia was answering in monosyllables. Phyllis returned to the kitchen and put the kettle on again.

'No,' Sophia was saying, still in this husky, unnatural voice. 'No . . . There's no point, Bron . . . Absolutely not . . . I'm sorry.' She was pulling at the paper towels with one hand. Phyllis saw herself helping her, tearing off a towel and offering it, but couldn't move. 'They're in the airing cupboard,' Sophia said. 'Top left-hand corner. You'll have to put the washing machine on tonight . . . Is she?' Her face flooded with colour and tears, but her voice became harsher. 'Well. I'm sorry. That's the way it goes . . . No. I told you. There's no point. *I don't want to talk about it!*' She slammed down the receiver, was silent for a moment, then started to howl like a wounded dog. It was a terrible sound. She doubled up, with her head in her hands, rocking and howling. Phyllis felt the weak tears come to her own eyes. She was nothing. She was worse than nothing. She couldn't even look after her own child.

At half past six, thank heavens, Sophia suggested they watched television. She seemed exhausted. Phyllis sat on the edge of her chair, hands in her lap, facing, without her glasses, the changing shapes and colours; Sophia also seemed to be staring at it without watching, except that when a baby or a small child came on she tore at the remaining paper towels and blew her nose with unnecessary vigour. At eight Bron phoned again, and again Phyllis tried to right herself after the blow of it not being Fred. She felt punch-drunk, silly. Sophia's voice was now clearer, but she still insisted that no, there was no point. She listened, though, while Bron was telling her about putting the children to bed. Phyllis knew this must be what he was telling her because she actually sounded proud when she said, 'Well, he's very sensible ... Did you wash his hair? ... Oh, good. That's great ... Yes. All right. If you like.'

It would be so wonderful, such a miraculous blessing if Sophia offered to get the supper. But she sat staring at the screen, quite limp, and of course Phyllis would never ask her. She burned both toast and scrambled eggs, the plates were smeared with ash, she just put them on the table without mats, glasses, candles, anything, and sat down in front of hers with a bump, feeling dreadfully giddy. Sophia didn't seem to notice. Chewing, she picked up Fred's bill and scanned it.

'What on earth's this? Bathroom and floorboards fifteen hundred pounds?'

'What?' Phyllis asked vaguely.

'How can you possibly spend fifteen hundred pounds on a bathroom? You didn't have a new bath, did you? What's it for?'

'Fifteen hundred pounds?' Phyllis asked, dazed. 'Is that what it says?'

'Honestly, Mother.' For a moment she sounded quite normal. 'Haven't you seen it? "For services rendered re bathroom and floorboards: fifteen bloody hundred pounds."'

'Oh,' Phyllis said. 'Oh.' Tears spilled out of her eyes. She made little squeaking sounds, fighting with herself. She grabbed the paper towels angrily, and tore off the last shreds.

'Are you all right, Mum?' Sophia asked, seeing her for the first time. 'Are you okay? I didn't mean to upset you, honestly. I'm sorry about all this, but honestly you mustn't be upset. Don't cry, it'll all turn out all right in the end, please don't cry . . .'

'Silly,' Phyllis mumbled. 'Don't take any notice. Just silly. It's a bit of a shock. I'm just *silly* . . .'

She longed to go to bed. Perhaps tomorrow would be better. If only she could be invisible. She couldn't, of course, go to bed. She couldn't leave Sophia alone in the bleak kitchen. There wasn't even a fire. She should make Sophia a hot water bottle. Tuck her up. Make cocoa, she did at least love cocoa. But it was impossible to make a hot water bottle and tuck that large young woman into bed and give her cocoa. How she wished it were possible. How she longed, painfully longed, to be able to do that, but she didn't have the will or the strength. Fifteen hundred pounds. It was a fortune. Supposing she didn't pay it? Fred must come and explain; she would write to him tomorrow, which was going to be better.

'Can I call Bron?' Sophia asked. She sounded determined.

'Yes, dear. Yes, of course.' 'For services rendered . . .' What did he mean by that? Was she worth fifteen hundred pounds to him, old bag of aching bones that she was? It was too horrible. Horrible, horrible. Shuddering, she stared at the screen without realizing that the television had been turned off.

'All right, then,' she remotely heard Sophia saying. 'If you insist. It won't do any good, though . . . Yes, of course . . . No, that'll be fine . . . Yes, I'm sure she will . . . Right.' She put down the receiver without saying good-bye. Phyllis looked up, searching for her.

'Well,' Sophia said. 'He insists on coming down tomorrow.'

'Here?'

'He's going to try and talk me out of it,' Sophia said proudly.

'But what about the children?'

'Oh, you'll look after them, won't you. It'll do you good.' She actually smiled. 'It's a black cloud,' said Sophia, 'that has no silver lining.'

Phyllis woke half a dozen times in the night. Each time, she was shivering more uncontrollably, her heart pounding faster. Was she ill? No, she was terrified. What of, you silly old creature? Not Fred. No, she would almost welcome Fred. She was terrified of the approaching day. Of her little grand-children, their merciless eyes, which weren't turned inwards, like Sophia's, their greed, their ruthless clamping on to her old love. She knew she would let them down; probably actually drop them on stones or in the mud. She couldn't feed them. She couldn't play Peter Rabbit and topple bricks. She must find a way out, a way out.

Perhaps she could run away, leaving a note. Let them sort it all out in her house, she didn't mind, let them stay for ever. But supposing they had another quarrel and Bron flung out? Or both of them (in opposite directions)? Suppose the children were abandoned? Or if Sophia grabbed Selina and made off, pursued by Bron? She saw Jasper standing on the path, alone and bewildered. None of this, of course, would happen. But what if it did? Or something worse?

No, she couldn't run away. Not yet, anyway. She must stick it out. Oh please, God, I really can't. She pulled her knees up to her chin, wrapped her arms round them, making a child-sized heap under the bedclothes. Her grey hair straggled over the pillow. Her face, intensely concentrated, was loose and crumpled, as though all its bones had collapsed overnight.

Nevertheless, somehow (so much of herself had become a mystery, she was amazed at watching herself cleaning her teeth, brushing her hair), somehow she got up and made breakfast and took Sophia a tray and swept the kitchen and washed up last night's dishes. She even looked tidy – pale, fearfully haggard, but tidy. When they arrived – Bron carrying Selina, Jasper walking cautiously up the path, not sure what he was going to find – she opened the front door and squatted on her heels, her arms wide to greet her dubious grandson.

'Is this where you live?' he asked.

'Certainly. Certainly it is.'

Clasped, he looked over her shoulder, still unsure. She picked him up, the great weight, and welcomed Bron, who looked terrible. Selina stared at her with the calm, judicious eyes she had dreaded. Selina was immaculate, completely beautiful. She was the most frightening of them all.

Sophia came down the stairs as they trickled into the kitchen, Jasper hanging back, Bron ducking Selina's head under the beams. The room was immediately overcrowded. Jasper, reassured, scuttled under the table, climbed over the wingchair to fling himself at his mother. It was all exclamations, embracing arms, eyes flickering here and there, and yet so silent that the little noises couldn't contend with it and petered out.

'Have you had breakfast?' Sophia asked. Now, suddenly, she was in command. This was her territory. Phyllis was accidental.

'Yes, thanks,' Bron said. He sat Selina down in the wing-chair and started undoing her jacket. She, having taken many minutes to size the matter up, held out her arms to Sophia and arranged her face in an expression of mounting grief. Sophia dived between them, pushing Bron out of the way. She held Selina close, rocking her, kissing the top of her silky head. 'It's all right,' she crooned. 'It's all right, baby, Mummy's here,' so gratifying Selina that the child broke into high, whooping wails, and choked and gasped and wailed in the intervals, and shuddered with dreadful sobs while Sophia walked up and down, up and down the two yards of clear space, rocking her and crooning. Jasper, disassociating himself, sat down to read last month's *House and Garden*. Bron looked hopeless. Phyllis wanted to cover her ears. At least – it was like the last thought of a drowning woman – at least the sun is shining.

Everything finally got sorted out. The toys were brought

from the attic. Chocolate biscuits were dispensed, though against Sophia's wishes. 'Well?' Sophia asked Bron, without looking at him. 'Would you like to see round the garden?' As though it were her garden, though she hadn't set foot in it yet. Never mind. 'Yes, do that,' Phyllis said eagerly. 'We'll be quite all right. It's a nice day – why don't you go for a walk?' Neither of them seemed to hear her. They were set on their struggle. The door closed, and she was responsible.

Jasper, pottering round the room, asked a few reasonable questions: why had she got that old table instead of the one she used to have; why did the floor have such big holes in it; where was the sitting room, if this was the kitchen; or, since they were sitting in it, where was the kitchen? He would like to see upstairs. Why did she have a door at the bottom of her stairs, nobody else did; where would he and Selina sleep if they had to stay; why was her bathroom downstairs, nobody else's was? There was nothing critical or complaining in his questions. It was a short inquisition, that's all. Finally satisfied, he sat down with his legs neatly dangling, waiting for the next occupation. Selina heaved a great sigh. She seemed to be wondering whether it was worth wailing again, since only her grandmother was there.

Phyllis looked out of the back door. Sophia and Bron were walking up and down by the stream. Why couldn't they either keep still or walk somewhere with a purpose? Sophia's head was down, she was hugging herself. Bron was gesticulating, making his points. She obviously mustn't disturb them for at least another hour. Jasper, feeling the need to rearrange something, had picked Selina up, staggered with her a few feet and dropped her with a thump. Selina, after a moment's consideration, decided she was injured. That at least took up ten minutes.

'I tell you what,' Phyllis said, desperately inventive. 'Why don't we go for a walk?'

'Where to? Have you got a park?'

'No, I haven't got a park. You don't need parks in the country. We'll go ... well, let's just go, anyway.'

'What about them?' He jerked his head in the direction of the back door.

'They're quite happy. They're just having a little talk.'

'What are they talking about?'

Dismayed, she heard herself say, 'It's no business of yours what they're talking about. Put these mugs in the sink. We're going.'

She had to get Selina's pushchair out of Bron's car – thank goodness he hadn't locked it, though it was a temptation to the Brig Boys – and put it together, with Jasper's advice, and strap Selina into it. Then they set off up the hill, Selina content with her regal position, Jasper with his hands in his jeans pockets, looking around benignly as though to say it wasn't such a bad old place after all. Suddenly, as they rounded the corner, he stopped dead, staring up and turning his head across the arc of the sky.

'What is it?' Phyllis asked, peering. 'An aeroplane?'

'Chiffchaff,' he said, and walked on.

'I don't think I know the chiffchaff,' presuming it must be a bird.

'*Phylloscopus collybita*,' he said casually, throwing a stone at the bank.

'Indeed,' she said, without smiling. She felt like an old woman pushing a rickshaw, though thought they were possibly pulled. Ancient, anyway; subservient and of no account.

When they reached Rebecca Broune's gate, she decided they were going to see Isabel. She wheeled the pushchair round, held it while she struggled to open the gate.

'Where are we going?'

'To see a friend of mine.'

'You said we were going for a walk.'

'So we are.'

'Lina doesn't like strangers.'

'Then,' this other voice said, 'she'll have to put up with it.'

She bumped the pushchair round to the back of the house, Selina passive as a holy image. Rebecca, of course, was among her roses. Thank heavens, Isabel was sitting on the terrace. She jumped up with a soft cry of welcome.

'I'm so glad to see you. It seems such a long time since Wednesday. I've tried to draw John's cenotaph. Are these your grandchildren?'

'Yes,' Phyllis said, prepared to hand them over.

Isabel looked at Jasper. 'Do you like it here?'

'I saw a chiffchaff,' he said uncomfortably.

'Won't you take her out of her pram?'

'Pushchair,' Jasper said. 'She'd better stay in it. She feels safer.'

So safe, in fact, did Selina feel that she had gone to sleep, slouched over the straps more dead than alive. Isabel eased the pushchair carefully up the steps, placed it in the shade of the plum tree and put the brake on. Jasper perched on the terrace wall. They were going to sit about again. Rebecca glanced up, but turned her back and went on with the weeding.

'They arrived unexpectedly,' Phyllis said.

'You don't look well.'

'I'm all right.'

'I feel so much better.'

'Good. Good, I'm so glad.'

'I might go back to London.'

'Really. When?'

'I don't know. Not yet. Not for some time.'

Perhaps she could tell Isabel. But no, she was too tired. Too disgusted. Besides, it would be bad for the girl to have her faith shaken. Isabel did have faith, she could tell. She had anchored herself to Phyllis, God knows why, an unfortunate choice in the circumstances. Phyllis wanted to close her eyes, rest a little.

'What are you drawing?' Jasper asked, seeing charcoal and a drawing block.

'My mother.'

'Where is your mother?'

'Down there. Weeding.'

'Can I look?'

'If you like.'

Phyllis had shut out the world.

'That's not your mother.'

'Yes it is.'

'It doesn't look like her.'

'Well, then. You draw something.'

'No, thanks.'

There was silence. Phyllis opened her eyes with a flutter. Jasper was scuffing down the path, looking around. Isabel drawing.

'Goodness. I must have fallen asleep for a moment.'

'Why don't you? You look very tired.'

'No, no. I must get back and make the lunch.' But she didn't move.

'Have you heard from your son?' Isabel asked, making long strokes with the charcoal.

'Not since he went back. No.'

'He wrote to Mother.'

'Really?' She didn't care. At the moment, apart from a sense of absence, she didn't quite know who her son was.

'I think she was rather pleased.'

'Yes. I'm sure she was.'

Her eyelids dropped again. The charcoal squeaked on the paper. When she struggled to wake up – it wasn't over, after all, not nearly over, she must face it again – Jasper was talking to Rebecca. He was standing on the edge of the rose bed like a small boy on the edge of a pool, while Rebecca lunged about on her knees, looking up at him. What on earth could they be finding to say to each other? She saw shades of the prison house beginning to close about the growing Jasper: Rebecca, his quarrelling parents, his grandmother. How dreadful it all was. And Isabel with her gas, her morbid tomb. It was a wonder that the sun could shine so indifferently; that the hours, hanging back as they did, could move at all.

'Things are very perplexing sometimes,' she said.

'Yes. They are.'

Selina twitched ominously. She flung herself back in the pushchair and opened her eyes wide, no sign of sleep but outraged at the strange place in which she found herself. Her face darkened. All was suddenly hurry and flurry. It's all right, darling, we must go, come along Jasper, let's go and see Mummy, it's all right Selina, thank you Isabel, come *along* Jasper. She waved weakly at Rebecca the free, Rebecca the strong. Rebecca signalled a brief good-bye and turned her back again.

'I'll come and see you soon,' Isabel said, clinging.

'Yes, yes. I may be going away.' She had no idea what she meant. Bump bump down the steps, out into the lane.

'That woman said some of her roses are thousands of years old. It's not true, is it?'

'I don't know,' Phyllis said, pushing up the hill. 'It might be.'

'They can't have been growing there for thousands of years. The garden wasn't there then. It was all ice.'

'Well, perhaps she didn't mean ... I don't know, Jasper.'

He looked wounded. He was anxious to get back to his parents, who knew.

Sophia and Bron were at least sitting down, Sophia on the tree-stump, Bron at her feet. Phyllis guiltily released Jasper, who ran down the hill towards them. Sophia made no effort to move, but held out her hand. Phyllis knew she ought to change Selina's nappy, but the thought was awe-inspiring, impossible. She couldn't get the lunch, anyway, until Sophia took over. She sat down outside the back door with the child on her knee, waiting.

At last, in her own good time, Sophia climbed slowly up the hill, holding Jasper's hand. Bron followed. He had been chewing a grass and idly threw it away as he walked; not, Phyllis was relieved to see, violently. Sophia had been crying again, but she looked purged; Bron had the exalted expression of a man who had survived great danger, his voice was hushed, his movements gentle. They settled down outside the back door to attend to their children. Phyllis, giving in, painfully ashamed, gulped a glass of brandy. She stumbled round finding bread, cheese, tomatoes, pickle. She didn't call them but sat with her teeth and fists clenched, a little old woman in pain.

*

Nothing was said to her. Their plan was still vague. In the afternoon they took Jasper for a walk, leaving Selina asleep in Phyllis's bed. The weight and intensity of their discussion surrounded them in a solid block, moving about with them from place to place, taking up all the room. Phyllis sat in the wingchair, dozing, starting up sometimes in fear of Selina. But the child slept, dribbling a little on the pink sheet.

When they came back, it seemed they had decided. 'I've got to go back,' Sophia said. 'Bron understands.' For her second insane moment, Phyllis wanted to implore this tall, solemn daughter not to leave her alone. She longed to say 'Take me with you' and hide herself in Sophia's pocket, in the basket along with the nappies and rusks and beaker, taking up no space. But she said, 'I'm so glad, that's much the best thing.'

'Sophia told me about your bathroom,' Bron said. 'The man must be a crook. Do you want me to deal with him?'

'No – oh, no. I'm sure it must be a mistake. Don't you worry, Bron, you've got quite enough to deal with as it is.' She was again and again astounded by herself. If only they would go. If only they would stay. If only they would go.

At last, infinitely slowly, pausing to answer Jasper's questions, to change Selina yet again, to fit in some last-minute observations on the house and garden, to put away the toys, to collect their possessions, to linger, to have second thoughts, to decide which of the children would go in which car, to show proper reluctance, at last they processed down the path.

'Thanks, Mum,' Sophia said, holding her.

'Thanks, Phil,' Bron said, kissing her cheek.

She stood behind the closed gate, ready to wave. Selina was buckled in, Sophia settled herself at the wheel. Jasper knelt in the back of Bron's car, eager to see Cryck disappearing. The two engines started up simultaneously. They moved off without looking back, although Bron raised his hand in a kind of blessing.

They had come, emptied her out, and gone. She had hardly been touched by their actual problems. It was this realization that made her unrecognizable to herself. Phyllis had believed all these years that whatever else she wasn't – clever, beautiful, a strong personality – she was at least a good mother and grandmother, she had at least been a good wife. It had been her secret opinion that this was far superior to being clever. She had really held a very high opinion of herself. It was not only that she had failed Sophia, but she hadn't even tried. She had offered no advice, no comfort. Sophia's decision had been made alone, because there was no alternative; she would never come again, if she was in trouble. Mother had proved an illusion, most of all to herself. She could hear Sophia's thoughts: a dead loss.

The field, the tree-stump, the yard retained some of their animation and urgency long after the sound of their cars had died away. But their spirit faded with the light; the sound of their voices, which hung in the air, grew thin with the air. They had used the place as a convenient background and had already forgotten it. When Bron had chewed and thrown away the blade of grass it had been any blade of grass, anywhere. Chewed, thrown away, she lay on her bed thinking how strange, how odd. After all these years.

The next morning she wrote a note to Fred: 'Dear Mr Skerry, I am very surprised by your account. Perhaps you would call round one evening and explain it to me in detail. Yours sincerely, Phyllis Muspratt'. On Wednesday, when she had not heard from him, she telephoned Bamfield Glass Company and asked to speak to Mr Skerry. The man came back after a couple of minutes and asked who was calling. He came back the second time and said Mr Skerry was out.

She had been drinking since returning indoors on Sunday

evening – not indiscriminately, but with a certain ceremony, steadily, with purpose. Brandy – whisky, gin, it hardly mattered – had, she thought, less effect on her now than it did. Gerald might have said she could hold her drink better. Gerald might have said a lot of things. He was in no position to criticize. On Thursday she put on a clean dress, tied a headscarf over her neglected hair and drove with immense caution to Bamfield.

She saw him as she got out of the car. He was walking across the big yard, some papers in his hand. She called 'Fred!' and waved as he turned, the wave faltering quickly. He hurried across to her with the same hard, twisted face she had seen the other night. She tried to compose herself as he came, but found it impossible.

'What are you doing here?' he demanded. 'What the hell do you think you're doing?'

'You didn't answer my letter. You weren't in when I phoned.'

'You are not to phone me here – or write, for that matter. Creeping Jesus, who do you think you are?'

She backed up against the car, holding her hand to her cheek as though her head were ringing. He seemed to relent a little. 'I'll come round on Monday. How's that? Seven, as usual.' She nodded, having nothing to say. 'Right, then. Now turn yourself round and get out of here. Understand?'

She scrambled into the car. She was shaking. She had to turn and reverse, turn and reverse, before she could get out of the gate, then missed an oncoming lorry by a hairsbreadth. Nobody had ever spoken to her like that before. Ever. She was not weeping, but her breath came in great shuddering gasps. She had to stop. She couldn't drive any more. Traffic sped at her from both directions. She covered her face, made herself small behind the steering wheel. Oh God, she kept saying, oh God what have I come to.

The shock was so great that for the next three days she kept quiet, treating herself with great civility. Her drinks became medicinal. Unable to go to the hairdresser – she must not drive, she must keep quiet – she washed her own hair and set it in tight little curls. Her face looked so ghastly that she covered it in make-up, tracing the bow of her mouth with care, although the tip of the lipstick was too broad and smudged, so she rubbed it out and put on more. She walked about with small steps, wearing her pretty sandals. There was no one to see, but she saw herself and thought she looked dainty. Otherwise she hardly thought at all. The time before Sophia's arrival seemed another age; an old age, perhaps. She felt beyond age now, as though she had slipped over the edge of her life. She noticed the interruption of darkness, but very little more.

On Monday, for the first time in weeks, she made an effort not to drink. She knew it was bad for her in some way, or at least that it might make her less able to deal with Fred, though she had stopped having any moral objection to it. When he's gone, she said. Until then, careful. The result was that by six o'clock she could think of nothing else. She was shaking again. But she made herself put on Sophia's slacks first – they were very casual, after all, very comfortable – and made up her face to hide, she hoped, the ravages caused by what must be carelessness. Then, very formally, she had her brandy.

He came round the back, as usual, but without overalls or tools. He sat down, took a hard look at her, and said, 'You have a question about the bill.'

'Yes.' She was very prim. 'It seems excessive.'

'Excessive, does it?' He stretched himself out. She remembered his short legs, his hot, adhesive skin. She looked away. 'Not asking me if I'd like a drink this evening? You're at it, I see.'

'You know where it is,' she said coldly. 'Help yourself.'

'Very gracious, Mrs M.' He went into the kitchen, banged about unnecessarily, came out with his whisky and water in a glass, went back again, came out with the bottle of Scotch and the bottle of brandy, dumped them on the table. Then, without a word, sat down again. There was silence. He drained his glass and poured another. Finally he said, 'Well?'

'I don't understand – I cannot understand how the work in the bathroom –'

'And the floorboards. I told you they're seasoned elm.'

'And the floorboards can possibly amount to fifteen hundred pounds.'

'You don't?' He lay back. 'Well, to tell you the truth neither do I. It seemed – shall we say – a reasonable figure. Wear and tear, Mrs M.? Strain on the old back? You can afford it.'

She was outraged. But she must keep quiet. After a moment she began, 'That's hardly the point –' but he groaned enormously, covering his eyes in an exaggerated gesture. 'Please, Phil. Do me a favour. Cut the cackle. I'm a busy man.'

'Give me an itemized bill, then,' she said sharply. She poured herself another brandy with a trembling hand. The conviction that everything in her life, since Gerald's death, had been the most terrible mistake settled softly in her mind and spread, filling every corner.

He looked her up and down, pausing here and there. She accepted his look bravely, though it was painful. He shook his head with a sound much dryer than laughter. 'I don't know, Mrs M. You take the biscuit. You really do. Look at you. All you need's the mint sauce. That's not at all bad – mint sauce. Get it? No, you wouldn't.' He leant forward with his old, sunny grin. 'Tell you what. Strip off and we'll forget the whole thing.'

'What?' she said stupidly.

'You heard me. Strip off and we'll forget the whole thing.'

She was drifting about somewhere in a high, foggy place. It was a kind of echo that said, 'What do you want from me?'

'I like to see old women. My speciality, if you like. No problem. I won't touch you much. Not so's you'd notice, anyway.'

'You're mad,' she said.

'You're longing to,' he said, with his friendly smile.

She stumbled up and teetered into the kitchen. He heard her knocking things over. He glanced quickly round then sprawled back in his chair, loosening his tie. Birds on the wing, a couple of butterflies, very pleasant. He eased off his shoes with his feet, letting them fall on the brick. He finished his whisky.

She came out holding a cheque, which she pushed into his face. For Phyllis, she looked quite crazy. 'Go,' she said.

He hesitated for a moment, then took the cheque, read it, folded it neatly and put it in his pocket. He reached for his shoes, untied the laces, put them on, tied the laces in double bows. He tightened his tie, stood up, poured another whisky, drank it.

'Well,' he said, 'glad you think you're worth it. So long, Mrs M. Nice knowing you.' He ran limber down the steps, stopped to look at a poppy, went on round the corner of the house, drove away.

20

Phyllis said, 'I can't manage. I must move.'

'Yes, I see,' Michael said. He saw nothing. On his way home, midnight, and there was his mother sitting in her car under the lamp-post. Hatless, fast asleep, and when he woke her, drunk. If she hadn't left her lights on, he might never have noticed. He had put her down on the sofa as though she were something he had bought earlier in the day and would soon have to unwrap. He couldn't remember what she was. Must be a mistake.

'I realize that I should have waited,' Phyllis said. 'But I couldn't.'

'Yes. Yes, I see.' He strenuously tried to recognize her. 'Did something happen?'

'Yes. Fred Skerry assaulted me. Then I started drinking.'

'The fellow you were talking about?'

'Yes. The handyman.'

'Oh.'

There was a long silence. Michael scrubbed his forehead with the heels of his hands. She was looking at him patiently. 'I'm sorry,' he muttered. 'I don't know what to say.'

'That's all right. You don't have to say anything. If Gerald had been alive, of course I'd have gone to him.' She seemed to puzzle over this for a moment, then gave it up.

'I'll make some coffee,' he said.

'Thank you.'

She didn't move while he made the coffee. Not a tremor, nothing but a steady blink towards the gas fire, which he had switched on after putting her on the sofa. When he poured her coffee her eyes turned to the cup, but she didn't touch it.

'Tell me about it then.'

For an instant, something moved in her face. A kind of amusement, or memory.

'Sophia came at the weekend. She'd left Bron.'

'She'd done what?'

'Yes. She'd left Bron. But she went back with him on Sunday.'

'Did she know about this?'

'Oh no. I couldn't tell her. She had quite enough to think about.'

She relapsed again into her limp concentration, her distance.

'Well, then,' he said. 'What happened?'

She told him very distinctly, though her voice came from far away. She didn't hesitate. It was almost as though she were reciting, reading aloud from some remote text. There were no excuses.

'I thought perhaps I should live with other people. Perhaps in some kind of Home.'

'Good God, Mother, that's not necessary, you can't do that.'

'Oh, I think so. It never crossed my mind that I couldn't manage. I can't, though.'

Jesus Christ. If she'd weep, or struggle. She wasn't even asking for his advice. She was at the end of her tether, and that just happened to be in his flat, on his sofa, in the middle of a Monday night.

'Did you bring anything with you? Nightdress? Anything like that?'

She looked vaguely worried for a moment. 'No. I'm afraid I didn't. Never mind.'

'You'd better get some sleep. We'll think about it tomorrow. I'll put some clean sheets on the bed –'

'No. Please don't do that. I'm very happy here.' She was using archaic words, though they came to her very naturally. 'I'd rather stay here.'

He stood over her, helpless. 'At least you're not hurt. I mean, you're not –'

'No, no. I'm not hurt.' She searched for him. Ah, there he

was. 'I'm sorry to disturb you,' she said. 'It wasn't possible, you see, to go to Sophia.'

For the first time in his life, he wanted to gather up and hold her. Warmth dawned. His eyes, throat and arms ached with a painful thaw. She seemed to feel it and passively accept it, though her smile was a long way off. 'Thank you,' she said. She moved, making a vague gesture as though to take his hand; not finding it, her own dropped back to her lap.

He gave her a pyjama jacket and his dressing gown and put her in the bathroom while he made up the sofa. She waited for him to come back, sitting meekly on the toilet seat, enormously shrouded. She could walk a little more firmly now, but the journey back to the sitting room was very slow. Curled on her side under the blanket, she took up hardly any room. He sat in the empty space at the other end, awkwardly holding her hand. She still watched the fire; then her blinking grew slower and heavier; at last her eyes remained closed, her breathing became more regular, she was asleep.

Michael's intense curiosity about himself was over. Without realizing it, he didn't give himself a thought. He wasn't aware of thinking at all. He just sat there, sometimes stirred by an incomplete rush of feeling, sometimes not. When he came to rationalize it afterwards, to describe to himself and decorate the history of the night, he thought it was possibly the sensation of being born. He had, for the first time, no attachment to or knowledge of his father. That would return, but differently placed. A faint beat was transmitted from the old woman's hand to his. The process of dissolution continued minute by minute, hour by hour.

Phyllis woke to a weight on her body. Michael had fallen asleep at last and was slouched across her legs. His hand was still in hers, his left arm imprisoning her. She knew exactly where she was. Unable to move without waking him, she lay still, looking out. She had never felt more tranquil, more naturally at home. Shame, indignation, humiliation were still being hurried away, but their protests were getting much fainter; they would be gone any moment now. It was a first morning. She was awed by it.

He woke shaking his head, as though to rid it of a few last dreams. He sat up, rubbed his beard, smiled. 'Hullo, how do you feel?'

'Quite well. You must have had the most uncomfortable night, I'm afraid.'

'No – no. I'm fine. I'll make some breakfast.'

She tidied the sofa, but did not offer to do anything else. She sat calmly looking at the fire while he fried eggs and made toast. Then, obediently, she came and sat down.

'We must make a plan,' he said.

She nodded.

'I have to go into the office –'

'Of course.'

'But I'll get away early. We'll discuss it all this evening. Will you be all right?'

'Quite all right. These are excellent eggs.' She shot him a timid look, not apologizing, but not pressing her point. 'I shall enjoy it.'

He was afraid she might drink too much again, and briefly wondered whether he should hide the whisky and vodka; but if she wanted to get drunk there was a rack of wine in the kitchen, and anyway she only had to go down to the Off Licence.

'If you're sure to be here when I get back, I'll leave you my key.'

'I shan't go out,' she said. 'I'd much rather you kept it.'

He showered and dressed. When he came back she had cleared the table and stacked the plates by the sink, but not washed up. It was as though she were tidying up her own traces item by item, leaving the rest to him. He was glad of it. 'You won't do anything – you know, round the flat. A woman comes in tomorrow.'

'No,' she said. 'I won't do anything.'

'I've left my number by the phone, in case you want to call me.'

'I won't,' she said, 'but thank you for thinking of it.'

When he left, she was sitting at the table turning over the pages of a magazine.

He worried about her all day, telephoning her before lunch and again in the afternoon. Each time she said she was quite all right, very much better, but didn't tell him not to worry. He was distraught with Piers, absent-minded with an old, distinguished actor whose reminiscences would inflame no one. He signed a number of letters without reading them, scrawled over some and sent them back to be re-typed. He left the office at four, bought some fish and took a taxi home.

She was dressed, clean and, he was thankful to find, sober. She was writing something, and had been for some time, judging from the crumpled sheets of paper in the wastepaper basket.

'I thought I'd make a Will,' she said, tidying the paper, capping the pen. 'Somehow I never thought of it after Gerald died. Did you have a good day?'

He would like to have made a joke, but couldn't think of one.

'And I rang up Mr Hodgson – you remember? The Vicar? – to ask him if he knew of any private Homes in the area. I thought I should go back to Surrey. But he wasn't terribly helpful.'

'Did you speak to Sophia?'

'No, no. I can't do that. Not till everything's settled.'

He realized that he had been waiting for her to find him inadequate and turn to Sophia. Since she wouldn't, he went on changing, growing here, losing pieces of himself there, keeping his normal face over this revolution. He put the fish in the fridge and made a pot of tea. The opinion he was about to provide, whatever it was, would affect the rest of his mother's life. He thought she would abide by it. He knew that it had got to be sound, without prejudice. He also knew – and this was the most significant and extraordinary thing about it – that he would have an opinion. His impatience to discuss his mother's future was, therefore, considerably greater than hers. She was content, at the moment, simply to recognize its existence.

'The way I see it,' he said, settling himself down, 'is this.' He waited, but she just looked at him with interest, so he continued. 'You had a horrible shock. It was enough to upset anyone – well, anyone of your age. I could happily murder the man,' – he would have liked this truth to please her, but her expression remained unchanged – 'but that wouldn't do you any good. Or me, for that matter. What I'm trying to say is – it's not the end of the world.'

She continued to look very attentive. 'You must realize,' he said, 'that people have these shocks in their lives. Well, you yourself. Look how you dealt with Dad dying –'

'It was different,' she said quietly. 'He didn't do it on purpose. You said so yourself.'

'True.' He was prepared to be fair, but this was more judicial than he felt. 'It was a shock, nevertheless. You didn't panic. It was two and a half years before you decided to move. It wasn't a – whim, is what I'm trying to say. Now you've had another shock – maybe a worse one, in some ways. But it's thrown you. You've – well, you've panicked. Isn't that so?'

'It was,' she said. 'I'm not in a panic now.'

'No. Well, that's fine. You still need a lot of time before you can come to a decision that will affect the rest of your life. And,' he heard himself saying, 'a great deal of mine.'

She looked away for a moment, then back at him, composed.

'What I suggest,' he went on, listening to himself with astonishment, 'is that you give yourself the rest of the summer. Give it another try. If you still feel you want to leave Cryck in September, October, you'll have had time to think of a sensible alternative. I'm sure you'd regret any decision you took now.'

'But I don't want to go back,' she said reasonably.

'Right.' This had to be considered, after all. He tried, again for the first time in his life, to put himself in her position. 'What's the alternative? You don't want to go to Sophia?'

'No.'

'And I'm afraid you can't stay here. The sofa would pall on both of us after a bit.'

'I wouldn't dream of staying here,' she said gently.

'You could go to an hotel. But you know what you are, when you're – well, when you're in your normal state. Always fussing with this and that. What would you do in an hotel? You couldn't cook, clean, rearrange the furniture. You wouldn't have a garden. You couldn't have people to stay – unless, of course, they could afford it, and I can't see Bron affording a weekend in Brighton for the entire family. All this is equally true of some private Home, or whatever it is you've been thinking of. It would kill you. In no time at all. Kill you.'

Until he saw how wide her eyes had become, he didn't hear the conviction – yes, the passion – in his voice. The idea of his mother in an institution, however comfortable and costly, was far worse than the thought of her death. Besides, she was so energetic, so able. 'You could travel, I suppose,' he said, making an effort to control himself.

'I've no particular wish,' she said, as a matter of fact, 'to travel.'

'Well, then.' He clasped and unclasped his hands, hitting them together. 'I suggest I take you back to Cryck on Thursday. I can take a couple of days off, that's no problem. If you want me to go and see this fellow, to make sure he won't molest you again –'

'It wasn't just Fred,' she said thoughtfully. 'I've never really settled. The people aren't friendly. I'd hoped to be active, but I'm lonely. I don't manage well. Fred was just – well, Fred was the last straw, that's all.'

'What about Rebecca and her daughter – what's her name – Isabel?'

'Isabel's very friendly. We had a nice time the other day, except that she fell in love with some morbid tomb in the

Abbey. Rebecca ... It's funny. I feel now as though I know her very well. But she doesn't know that. She doesn't like me. I don't like her. There you are. It's funny.'

'Yes,' he said, trying to understand her; understanding her. 'Yes.'

'Sometimes I feel that I'm not really there. I dress myself, feed myself, put myself to bed, get myself up again. But it's as though –' – she frowned, trying to think of an image that would serve – 'as though I'm doing all those things to a doll. You understand? Not quite like that. But rather pointless, just the same.'

He thought of saying that most people's lives were pointless – his own, for instance. But that was irrelevant. 'I don't know the solution to that,' he said.

'No. Neither do I.'

'There wouldn't be any more point if you lived in a Home, would there?'

'No. But having other people to talk to would make it seem as though there was.'

'Yes.' In the same way that his friends gave him a purpose. 'I see that.'

They had reached a natural pause. He got up and walked over to the window, looked out, saw nothing, turned and came back. She didn't seem quite as passive as she had done; she was frowning slightly, trying to puzzle things out.

'You've only been there a few weeks,' he said.

'Two months. It's not very long, I know.'

'You're bound to make friends. You always do.'

'That's what I thought,' she said patiently.

'You must have had a good reason for leaving Surrey.'

'Not very. I think it was something to do with the plums.'

She had never said anything to him about plums. He hadn't asked her. He saw the immensity of everything he had to learn. It wasn't at all clear or specific, simply a feeling of great ignorance, and a desire to find out. 'Plums,' he said. 'Well, I suppose that's good enough.'

'Not really.'

'No. Well. First things first, yes? I'll come down as often as I can.'

She turned in her chair, her face pitiful. 'No!' she protested, distressed for the first time. 'That isn't why I came! That isn't what I want! I'm not an invalid. I won't have it!'

'I'd like to,' he said simply.

That was all. Take it or leave it. He sat down again, and waited.

She thought for a long time, staring at the extended fingers of her left hand, turning her wedding ring round and round. To Michael, his argument seemed conclusive. She appeared to be accepting some of it, discarding some, doubting some. Apart from the fact that she didn't have her glasses on, she looked as though she were playing Patience. At last she sighed shortly, put her hand away, looked up at him.

'Very well,' she said. 'I'll give it another try. For the summer.'

21

The return to Cryck wasn't easy. During the remainder of her stay in London Phyllis had allowed herself to be looked after, as though this was now her right; for her son it was a necessary exercise which he performed gratefully, with a natural skill that surprised him. Once back in Cryck, she was troubled again, nagged by memories of duty and obligation. She was very clumsy. Her darting about was aimless. She was always on the point of remembering some purpose, but never found it. Fuss seemed imminent. He was helpless in the face of these old habits and waited patiently for her to find her feet. The surroundings reminded her to start drinking again, but she very often forgot and sat unoccupied. She had withdrawn into herself and he didn't know what was happening there. He was watchful, but did not comment. The important thing was that he should be with her when she reached a decision.

He was, therefore, worried about leaving her. He thought he knew better than to expose her to Rebecca, but on Sunday afternoon, while Phyllis was sleeping, he went with some reluctance to talk to Isabel. The girl – woman, person, whatever she was – didn't seem pleased to see him.

'Mother's in the garden – I'll call her.'

'I came to see you, actually.'

'Me?' Her small eyes, sparsely fringed with sand, were hard with suspicion. 'What for?'

'I think you can help, if you will.'

'Help?'

He looked round the dark sitting room. It was filthy, cluttered with books and flower pots and old newspapers. 'Could we sit down?'

'If you like.' But she didn't, hovering. 'Mother won't understand. You'll have to explain.'

'Are you so frightened of her?' he asked dryly.

She was stiff, giving nothing away. He explained the situation. As he told her everything, she moved slowly towards a chair, at last settled on it, her hands folded. 'So you see,' he said, 'I'm worried about leaving her. I'll come down as much as I can, but I can't come every weekend. I don't know what's going on at the moment. She's not talking. I'd like you to keep an eye on her.'

There was a long silence. She stared at him incredulously. Although he knew she had believed what he told her, he wondered whether she had understood; or perhaps it was too much for her to cope with. 'Yes,' she said finally. 'Of course.' There was another silence. Then, as though there was no need for further discussion, 'What shall I tell Mother?'

'Do you have to tell her anything?' he asked irritably. 'It's not her business.'

'No.' She looked downwards, sideways, picked up a paper-clip, inspected it, turning it over and over. 'She'd enjoy it,' she said.

Michael found her obsession distasteful. He snapped childishly, 'I'm thinking about my own mother, not yours. Rebecca can look after herself.'

That evening he asked Phyllis, 'What d'you think of Isabel?'

'Isabel?' For a moment she seemed not to remember who Isabel was. 'Oh. I think she's quite a nice girl, really. Rather too demanding.'

'She seems anything but demanding. What do you mean?'

'I don't know.' She thought for a few moments, again – a recent habit – twisting her wedding ring. 'I suppose if you're deprived ... you make a lot of demands? Isn't that so?'

'But do you trust her?'

'Trust her? What an odd question. I really haven't thought about it.' So she did, looking at Isabel this way and that. 'Yes,' she concluded, 'I think I'd trust her. But I'm not sure whether you mean with the teaspoons or with ... in a larger sense.'

'Well, I hope you see a bit more of her. Take her on another outing.'

'I'd like to, but not to the Abbey. We'll think of somewhere more cheerful next time.' She shot him a canny look. 'Have you asked her to keep an eye on me?'

'Well. In a way.'

'Just so long as I know. I'm not very good at being looked at just now.'

'But you won't avoid her?'

'Oh no. On the contrary. I quite enjoy her company, so long as she doesn't expect too much.'

He wasn't reassured. On the other hand he had to get back to work. His life up until Monday night seemed an uneventful childhood, its discomforts largely imagined; it had been pleasant, comfortable, and tedious. There was now so much to deal with, quite apart from his mother, that he felt impatient and preoccupied, unable to be in two places at once, wanting to be in several. He left on Monday morning, promising to return the following weekend.

*

Phyllis took up her life again. It was, she thought, only temporary. She wrote to various private Homes and received two glossy brochures by return, which she read with interest. It seemed that she would have to turn everything over to these people, though a proportion of it, they said, would be recoverable on her death. It would certainly be a placid life, not unlike entering a convent, though a great deal more expensive. She doubted whether a convent would take her, since her faith was not really worth much. And it was no good pretending that she didn't like to be comfortable. The company of other old ladies and gentlemen with similar pasts to her own, the exchange of children and grandchildren by means of fading photographs, the relinquishing of love and all its agitation, were priceless benefits. She would have to delay finalizing her Will until she found the right place, but in the meanwhile she must put her house in order.

Her house was already in order. That was frustrating. She

must, then, accumulate some pleasant experiences to store up for the future. Enlisting Isabel, she embarked on a programme designed to last over the summer. She intended to see bamboo groves, grottoes, canals, ha-has, temples, lakes, potagers and parterres; she made an extensive list of birthplaces, Roman remains, agricultural museums, Plantagenet manor houses and baroque palaces; wild life was not overlooked, nor were demonstrations of falconry and Morris dancing, but she wouldn't go to any more abbeys or cathedrals or have anything to do with bones, human or dinosaur. 'The past is all very well,' she told Isabel, 'provided there are still people in it.' Traipsing across the floor of a Roman villa on a wet Thursday, peering at bits of mosaic in the grass, Isabel asked where the people were here. 'All about,' said Phyllis inconsistently, indicating a coach-load of damp tourists. 'Anyway, this place was at least lived in.'

'So was John Wakeman,' Isabel said.

At the weekend, Phyllis showed Michael her plan. Not altogether understanding her purpose, he thought it showed a very catholic taste but that she might do better to concentrate on fewer interests. A trout farm and Chinese wallpaper in one afternoon seemed, to his editorial mind, a bit haphazard. He was afraid she would tire herself. He wished her plans included staying at home more often. She was in the process of emancipating herself from home, but told him there would be plenty of time for that in the winter. In the meanwhile, she said, she had to consider Isabel as well as herself. The girl appeared to be artistic, and might enjoy Chinese wallpaper; she herself preferred trout. Her argument seemed to Michael illogical, but that was only to be expected. She was making progress, that was the main thing. He lent her his camera so that she could snap trout and the other living things she preferred.

*

In the meanwhile Rebecca, in her own image, lay doggo; she

watched, occasionally growled, twitched off the odd irritation, went on watching. Something was happening; she smelled change; her comfort was disturbed by distant anticipation, like the first stirrings of hunger.

Michael always took his summer holiday in August – a drab, worn-out month, but a time when he was particularly welcomed by his friends. He shepherded them round Naples and Marrakesh, played cricket on inclement beaches, took them out to dinner in Malaga, cooked for them in Aird. Alone with their families, the men tended to become restless, the women plaintive, the children more or less rebellious according to age; the first thing they did after renting their villas, hotels, cottages or pensions was to secure Michael for as much time as he could spare.

This year he was committed to Grasse, Brittany and Llanbedrog. In a few idle moments at the office, without giving it much thought, he cancelled them all. He would spend a bit of time in Cryck, then wander off on his own somewhere. He was no longer a surrogate. He knew the consternation he had caused and was apologetic but not remorseful.

It was over six weeks since Phyllis had turned up at his flat. He had spent three weekends at the cottage, and she seemed to have made what she herself called a remarkable recovery. He didn't know whether it was the change in himself – which he recognized as a boy recognizes puberty, or a man the sudden functioning of a dead limb – or in her that had altered their relationship. It didn't matter. She was easy with him, almost indifferent; he indulged and cared for this new, independent spirit that required neither indulgence nor consideration. She seemed to be aiming at some distant target. She stopped her incessant sight-seeing over these weekends, though didn't disguise her reluctance at doing so. Ruefully, she said she still had a few manners left. He was glad to be the reason for keeping her at home occasionally, making her think about food and laundry, pinning her down.

He had a slight dread of her expecting him to accompany

her on these expeditions, if he stayed for longer, but realized with relief that he needn't have worried. 'Isabel and I get on very well,' she said. 'We're both learning a great deal and I think you'd put her off. You could get something for supper, though, if you happen to go to Lamberts Heath.' She didn't often bring Isabel home with her – he got the impression that Isabel slightly resented his presence – and in the evenings Phyllis would tell him about potteries or Palladian villas; sometimes they casually compared their pasts, making a composite picture of Gerald as husband and father which mildly surprised both of them; Sophia was touched on only occasionally, more often as a girl than as a woman since they were both excluded from her present life; by unspoken but conscious mutual agreement they never discussed Rebecca or Isabel and never referred to the future. He hoped that as day by day she assimilated the future, docketing it away in the past, she would grow less frightened of it. She, hoarding the present, putting herself in order, was not in the least frightened. This was their only misunderstanding.

One morning Phyllis set off very early, equipped with provisions and an itinerary designed to please – and, Michael suggested, totally exhaust – both Isabel and herself. He cleared up a bit, wrote some letters, cut the lawn, listened to a lunchtime concert on the radio. In the afternoon, as usual, it began to rain. He thanked God he wasn't building sandcastles in St Malo, but he was a naturally gregarious man and was also beginning to feel that he was wasting time. He wasn't sure what he wanted, but he was impatient for action of some sort. The secretive village, each house and cottage a fortress, bored and irritated him. He could understand his mother feeling lonely, even going a little crazy. Something must be done about that. He used this, rather than his own curiosity, as a reason for going to see Rebecca.

She was working outside, wearing a filthy army jacket which at first camouflaged her among the shrubs. The rain had plastered her hair to her skull; with her dark glasses and sodden cigarette she looked like an old, blind labourer.

'Well,' she said. 'I've been expecting you.'

'I've been meaning to come.' He felt he had to raise his voice. Did the woman never go indoors? He was soaking. 'Am I interrupting you?'

'Yes, but it doesn't matter.' She wrenched off a wet branch and threw it to one side. 'We'd better go in, I suppose.'

On their way back to the house, she opened the door of a small, broken-down building – an old storehouse, perhaps, or outside washroom – and dropped her armful of shears, scythe and rake inside. She was about to slam the door when he saw rows of bookshelves in the gloom. 'What's that?' he asked, peering.

'Nothing. Just a rubbish dump.'

'But you've got books in there. Can I see?' He pushed past her, stepping in. The room – or it had, at one time, been a room – seemed much larger inside; half the back wall, invisible from the garden, had been made into a window that looked down over the valley; the other walls were lined with books – the top shelves would need a ladder to reach them, but there was no ladder; a huge surface in front of the window, supported on bricks, was piled with old papers, more books, bags of potting compost, broken seed trays, secateurs; almost hidden under all this was a large, old-fashioned upright typewriter. Posters, book jackets, clippings and photographs once pinned to the sides of the shelves now mostly hung by one pin, all were mottled and faded. The floor was grey with dirt and crunched underfoot. Spiders had curtained the corners of the window, against which the rain beat and drizzled. The place smelled damper than a cellar, dustier than an attic at mid-day.

'My work room,' Rebecca said. 'Like it?' When Michael said nothing, she stepped outside, holding the door open. 'Let's go up to the house.'

'Can't we stay here?'

After a moment's hesitation she shrugged, and shut

the door. 'Your interest is morbid,' she said. 'But go ahead.'

'Go ahead?'

'Nose about, if you want to. That's why you came, after all.' She flourished her smoking fingers towards a bookshelf. ' "Works of" are there. No room for more, thank God.' She pretended to ignore him, drying the shears with what looked like an old cushion cover.

'You think I came to spy on you?'

'Probably. You're my publisher, after all. I owe you a great deal of money.'

'Then let's go up to the house.'

'No, you can stay if you want to.' She worried the corner of the cushion cover into an uncapped jar of vaseline and started anointing the scythe.

He moved slowly round the room, craning to see the books, peering at the memorabilia. Except for the lack of musicology, it was a library he would have liked to own.

'Why don't you write any more?' he asked casually, his back to her.

'Because I don't want to,' she answered just as casually.

'A pity.'

There was silence except for the industrious polishing. Then she asked, 'Who for?'

'The people who like reading you,' he said, too blandly.

She cackled. 'I'm disappointed in you, Muspratt. What kind of a name is that, anyway? Muspratt. You know damn well that if they can't read me, they'll read someone else and never know the difference.'

'Well. I didn't mean it.' He looked round for something to sit on, but apart from the upturned packing case occupied by Rebecca there was nothing. 'What d'you want me to say – English literature?'

'I don't *want* you to say anything. If you must, you can at least say what you mean.'

'All right, then. It's a pity for you.'

'What the hell do you find to pity about *me*? Apart from

one or two minor irritations, I'm probably the most contented person you know –'

'Irritations like Isabel?'

'For God's sake let's not talk about *Isabel*. Leave that to your mother.'

'You don't like my mother.'

'Not particularly. I don't dislike her. Does that offend you?'

'No. She doesn't like you either. But she says she feels she knows you very well.'

'Knows *me*?' Rebecca whooped, kicking her heels. 'Well, I hope she enjoys it.'

'Don't you? Enjoy it, I mean?'

She plunged her hands in her pockets and stared at him. Then, ominously calm, she asked, 'Is this the way you usually talk to your writers? Are you serious?'

'I just wish you'd write another book. That's all.'

'Jesus Christ!' Her anger struck so suddenly that he almost lost his footing. 'Jesus bloody Christ, Muspratt! I've written God knows how many fucking books, and a million words of crap! I've had three husbands, lovers before you were born, kids, gas, electricity, waters broken, pipes burst – I've made more money than you'll ever see and spent the lot! I'm an old woman, Muspratt! I like to garden! What have *you* done with your life?'

He stared at her. In the past, he would have crumpled. He could even hear himself saying, 'I'm sorry – forget it.' Instead, sounding as wondering as he felt, he said, 'You're scared stiff,' not realizing until after he had said it how stiff she actually was, rigid and blazing.

'I'm *what*?'

'Frightened. Out of your wits – literally.'

Rebecca elaborately composed herself, finding a tolerant smile and wearing it anyhow. She took an unnecessarily long time searching for and lighting a cigarette. 'Do please continue,' she said with childish sarcasm.

It was no good pretending he wasn't nervous. He even

glanced apprehensively at the sharp instruments that surrounded her. But passion had again taken hold. He walked
three steps up and down as he spoke, using his hands to offer
words. 'I don't know what your intention was, hiding yourself
down here, but I can guess – you were getting old, you didn't
want to be seen, watched, talked about, maybe ridiculed.
Your writing, after all, was very much an expression of your
personality – I mean that some people's writing *is* their personality, they have nothing else, but not you. You – well, you
ate your own life. I'm not saying it wasn't seasoned with other
things, you understand. You didn't always like the taste of it
– in fact one gets the impression that it often disgusted you,
but that's what made you good – excellent – sometimes great.'

If there was to be an interruption – he was no longer looking
at her closely – he didn't wait for it. 'But I think that as you
felt your active life – relationships and so on, your role as
Queen Bee, maybe sex – I'm sorry, I don't know about that
of course – I mean as you felt all that leaving you, you began
to fool yourself there was nothing left and you couldn't bear
that, the idea that anything you wrote might be scraping the
barrel, people pitying you. So you rationalized the whole thing
and decided to give up.'

'You may well be right,' she said drily. 'I don't care for your
metaphors, but you may well be right. So I've given up. Any
more revelations?'

'You haven't given up. You're just too frightened to go on.'

'Really.' She absurdly blew ash off the mud-caked sleeve of
her jacket.

'You're forgotten,' he said bitterly. 'Old hat. Missed the
bus. A has-been. Does that please you?'

'I don't care about it much.'

'But what about your own need, for God's sake –'

'What need?'

Perhaps she was being honest, after all. Maybe, as he'd
suddenly found himself believing, her creativity had been just
part of the liveliness of her youth. Maybe she was now just

any old woman, as simple as his mother; far more simple than his mother. 'What about the notebooks?' he asked.

'What notebooks?'

'You told me you only wrote notebooks.'

'I wonder why I told you that. Well. So I do.'

'What do you write in them?'

'None of your business.'

'I care. I don't know why. It's nothing to do with publishing you. I do care.'

'I think you do. But it's misplaced, my boy. You're flogging a dead horse.'

'Can I see one?'

'Of course not.' She stretched out her legs, sunk her chin on her chest and stared for some time at the toes of her rubber boots. The room, to Michael, became increasingly disturbed with her thoughts. 'They're on the shelf over the desk,' she said. She slumped further, brooding within.

He could hardly believe it. The eight-foot shelf was packed with spiral-backed notebooks, to him an inordinate treasure. Before she could change her mind he took one at random from the centre of the shelf, opened it. The entry was dated two years before, 15 May:

... Then came last Monday, working at last on something I had some faith in, and all seemed solved, satisfied. On Tuesday a block, but kept trying. Wednesday car wouldn't start etc. so did the Womens piece instead (torture – £200). Yesterday typed it, clipped bay, cut grass. Today woke with a bleakness not felt for years. You're dead, R B. Done for. Fear no substitute for hunger & thirst. All fear.

It won too easily. Yes, yes, & self-disgust as repellent as failure. I race rush to the garden but it steals me, makes impossible demands. My incompetence. All this will be forgotten if it's only a temporary lapse & not yet another 4 pages to lie about dying. But they have that pallor, already rained on. Canary Bird in bud.

He couldn't read any more. He closed the notebook and put it back. Rebecca didn't look up. He raised his hands and let them fall helplessly. It was no satisfaction to be proved right. On the contrary, he felt defeated.

'I've got nothing to say.'

'No?' She looked at him straight. Her face seemed smaller and sharper, blanched with effort. She stood up, still hugging the jacket round her. 'Good,' she said. 'Then perhaps you can leave me in peace.'

Phyllis had almost made up her mind. She had found a place near East Grinstead that would, she thought, suit her very nicely. She visited it after Michael left, telling no one, travelling by train and spending the night in a comfortable hotel. The Home – though it was merely called The Manor – had pleasant rooms, long narrow windows, elaborate chimney stacks; it was rosy with the first glow of Virginia creeper, hydrangeas in pots stood either side of the front door. Each two-roomed suite – there were, of course, bed-sitting rooms, but Phyllis smiled and said no, no they didn't interest her – had its own kitchenette and private telephone, though naturally there was a communal dining room and drawing rooms for those who wished to be sociable. It was apparently owned by an American company, but the couple who managed it were charming, exactly like hosts at the country house they had, on account of the exigencies of tax and inflation, been forced to leave. It had only been open a year, they said, so if Mrs Muspratt would care to pay a deposit – they hated asking her, but unfortunately these things had to be done – she could go top of the waiting list. They couldn't show her the actual suite at the moment, as it was occupied – Phyllis appreciated that this might be tactless, to say the least – but it was identical with the one next door, where Lord Blount, busy with his jigsaw, hardly acknowledged their presence once he realized that it wasn't his suite Mrs Muspratt was after.

After paying her deposit – it wasn't returnable, but she thought it worth the risk – and saying good-bye, Phyllis strolled in the gardens for a while. Two much older ladies, very neat in their heather-mix tweeds and pearls, reassuringly hatless to show they were at home, passed her in the rose garden, smiling creases in their well-powdered faces as they said good afternoon. An old gentleman creeping along with a walking stick commented that it was a very fine day. A gardener was cutting the grass. There was a distant tinkle of teacups through open downstairs windows. A uniformed maid hurried across the gravel carrying an air cushion. It was another era, another world – her own. She couldn't in any way, by the most tortuous efforts of her imagination, see Gerald here. Gerald, after all, would never grow old; compared with hers, his experience had been limited. Fred – her thoughts balked at the old ladies, scurried away – would never come here. Nor would the Brig Boys. Nor – she actually gave a little hiccough of laughter – would Rebecca Broune storm about in her dreadful clothes, polluting the air and scorning Fragrant Cloud and Grandpa Dickson. On the other hand, she could just see Jasper running across the lawn and Michael taking tea with her on the terrace. They would leave, of course, but that was what made it so safe. This was a place where one could gradually prepare, step by step, for dying, instead of being catapulted into it in the clumsy way that most people were, leaving dismay behind.

On her return to Cryck, the cottage seemed more unsuitable than ever. She couldn't think how she had ever convinced herself that she could live so unnaturally. It had been Sophia's choice, of course – a young woman's idea of how a grandmother should live, baking bread no doubt, gardening, knitting larger and larger jumpers as she sat by the cosy fire. Well, she was tired of baking, didn't really care for gardening, and the cosy fire had to be cleaned out and fuelled. After a lifetime of service, however willing it had been, she was prepared to be shamelessly selfish. Thanks to Gerald, there was no need to expose herself to any more danger. The greatest bequest she could make to Michael and Jasper, Sophia and Selina, was the memory of a well-cared-for, happy and independent old woman trotting off to death in the company of her peers.

But she knew there would be argument, both of her children misunderstanding her motives, so she kept quiet. There were a lot of legalities to arrange and she was in constant correspondence with Gerald's solicitor. The cottage had to be put on the market, but a surprising viciousness made her determine not to let the Brigadier know – the Brig Boys would never tramp across her field if she could help it. Even if she tried to sell it through a London estate agent, the Brigadier would smell it out. So she delayed until the present occupant of her suite at The Manor had, as they ambiguously called it, moved on; then she would put an advertisement in *The Times*. With the renovated bathroom (she deliberately refused to think of the £1,500, shutting her mind so tight that not the faintest tremor could escape), the place was already worth more than she had paid for it.

Everything, in fact, was very satisfactory. She felt more free and easy than she had done in the whole of her life. Her odd relationship with Isabel – it had seemed, for a while, a little odd – had established itself as a kind of friendship. The girl was so uncritical of her, though opinionated enough about architecture and landscape. Phyllis had even discussed Fred with her, though briefly. 'It's the fact that he gave you no choice,' Isabel said. 'That's what's unbearable – when you're not given the choice. That's why what happened to the Jews was so awful.' Phyllis couldn't believe that even if given the opportunity she would have chosen to be assaulted (though in that case, of course, it wouldn't have been an assault) by Fred, let alone that any Jew would have chosen to go to the gas chambers. Still, she recognized it as an opinion and perhaps there was something in it. Anyway Isabel's reaction was a lot easier to accept than the outrage she would have got from Sophia, if Sophia had known. That would simply have been embarrassing and distressing to them both.

Her new relationship with Michael filled her with peace, which the old one had never done. Asking his help in that time of extreme despair seemed to have enabled her to see him for the first time. Of course that couldn't be true, so perhaps it was he who had, as it were, become visible. Whatever the reason, they had become equals. He could even offend her now, with his impractical political views for instance. Now that she no longer needed him to deal with her affairs he was quite helpful. But none of that mattered any more. He had grown up and would probably even get married some day. The pleasure she felt in this was constant, and all the more pleasing for being remote.

Jasper was her only unresolved problem. She was still troubled by a feeling of having failed him on his only visit to Cryck – failed them all, in fact. It mattered most with Jasper because her love for him still had an urgency, a sense of the future, which didn't fit in with her schemes. In idle moments she could still feel piqued that Sophia didn't seem to think a grandmother was necessary to him; she still ached to impose treats and gifts, to bribe him away from Sophia's authority; she still wondered occasionally whether Bron's mother, though safely tucked away in New Zealand, wasn't putting in a sly bid for Jasper's favours. She knew it was irrational and unjust, but couldn't help feeling that Sophia and Bron were keeping Jasper away from her. She had dreamed of getting a bird table, hanging a coconut, making him fruit cakes to take away to school when the time came, except that of course he wouldn't be going away to school. Jasper was the only remaining link with her past and the only reason for extending it into the future. She had been a little too optimistic that day at The Manor. The thought of Jasper made her wonder if she might be thought a deserter.

However, Sophia very seldom phoned nowadays. She was probably ashamed of her collapse, silly girl, and never mentioned it. They had been abroad, Normandy or was it the Dordogne, for most of August. Now school had started again, and it was such a hassle to come just for a weekend. Believing that this was what Sophia felt, Phyllis managed not to ask her. Jasper was growing week by week, season by season, but Sophia had too much on her plate – again Phyllis heard her, and tried to understand – to think of packing him up and sending him off to Grandma. This little pain must be cured somehow. In the meanwhile, Grandma sent him picture postcards of the captive lions and adventure playgrounds he was missing.

It was a year since she had first seen the cottage. The plums were ripe again but she didn't, as she had intended, make jam. They were left to the wasps and Isabel, who stewed them. The leaves coloured and fell. The garden, a wilderness of michaelmas daisies and phlox, collapsed slowly; the dahlias' blackened stems lay about on frozen earth and the lettuce was slimy. Many historic houses, Flamingoland, dolphinaria, miniature railways, stately gardens and authentic wool dips closed for the winter. Phyllis and Isabel took up Italian, by means of gramophone records. Phyllis knew that she would never get beyond the conjugation of the most simple verbs, but Isabel was very quick. They sat by the fire and asked each other questions – *Di chi è figlio? Per chi è questo telegramma?* – giggling a good deal.

'*Fa degli esercizi fisici al mattino?*' Isabel inquired.

'*No, ma so fare un salto mortale,*' answered Phyllis fluently.

'*Io vado a Londra,*' Isabel said. 'I've got a job in a gallery, it starts next week.'

'What? I mean *come ha detto?* Doing what, exactly?'

'I don't know. More or less everything. It's a very small gallery, I shouldn't think anyone goes much.'

'Congratulations,' Phyllis said.

'*Tante grazie. Vorrei poter contraccambiare.*'

'I'm sorry?'

'I wish I could repay you,' Isabel said.

It seemed, somehow, a natural sequence to Isabel's decision that Phyllis should hear that her suite at The Manor was now available. There were a lot of formalities to complete, and of course they didn't wish to hurry her in any way. Christmas at The Manor was a very friendly affair, they made a really special effort to make their guests happy at that time, while of course avoiding the vulgarity so sadly associated with Christmas nowadays. But if she would prefer to join them in the New Year, that was perfectly all right. They would welcome her any time before January 17th, or on that day if it suited her better. They would like a short inventory of the furniture she proposed to bring, and enclosed a number of necessary forms which they would be grateful if she would return as soon as possible. Finally, they would like to say how glad they were that she was joining their little community – as Robert Browning so beautifully put it, 'Grow old along with me – the best is yet to be!' – and they were hers very sincerely.

She wished she could share the news with someone, it was so very exciting. Perhaps Isabel . . . ? But no, not until the girl was safely in London. She might let something slip, and although Michael didn't seem to be seeing anything of Rebecca, it wasn't worth the risk. The first thing to do was to sell the cottage – a sale couldn't be completed before Christmas, of course, but the bank in Surrey would certainly give her a bridging loan. She composed the advertisement, counting the words on her fingers, and sent it with a cheque to be inserted in both the Property and Personal columns of *The Times*; to foil the Brigadier she was vague – she hoped it couldn't be called misleading – about the location, and gave a Box number. Then she wrote to Dick, the present manager of Gerald's bank. To make doubly sure, she drove to Lamberts Heath and posted the letters there. When Isabel came round for their Italian hour, Phyllis contrived to turn the conversation towards Christmas,

'*Non posso soffrire* Christmas,' Isabel said. 'I hate it. Perhaps –' – such a look of hope – 'I'll come and stay with you.'

'I'm going away,' Phyllis said, purring.

'To stay with your daughter?'

'No. Italian, Isabel.'

'Then *quanto tempo intende fermarsi?*'

'I don't understand you, dear.'

'How long will you be away?'

Forefinger on lips, Phyllis leafed through her phrase book. '*Non ho nessun idea,*' she said triumphantly, with a bewildering smile.

'I came round, because there's rather a lot to explain.'

'I just can't get over it,' Sophia said.

'What?'

'How different you look without your beard. You've always had a beard.'

'Go on,' Bron said. 'A lot to explain about what?'

'Don't say you're getting married.'

'Could I,' Michael asked patiently, 'just begin?'

He found their house very uncomfortable and had only been there twice in the last six years. What was presumably intended as the adults' end of the sitting room was lit with a third-degree spotlight by which you could neither read nor, he imagined, thread a needle. It might well be the reason for the incessant headaches his sister complained about. There was a lot of reproduction art deco and the whole room had the feeling of being half moved into, or out of. The kitchen had a greater sense of permanence and he wished they could have stayed there, but Sophia had said she spent her life in it and having a guest was an excuse to be civilized for once.

He had a good reason for telling them what had been happening to Phyllis in the last few months and wanted to get to it as quickly as possible but Sophia would keep interrupting.

'You mean this awful attack happened the day before I went down there? But why didn't she *say*?'

'She probably thought you were a bit preoccupied,' Michael said drily.

'But if she'd only said! I thought she was upset, but of course I thought it was – well, me arriving like that. Poor little Mother. How perfectly ghastly. What an unspeakable brute. God, I feel *awful*.'

'I knew there was something fishy about that bill,' Bron said, 'but she wouldn't let me deal with it. What happened then?'

'She insisted on him coming round to explain and he said he'd forget it if she stripped off – it seems that's his thing, old women. So she paid it and came to me.'

'You?' Shock was following shock so rapidly that Sophia's normal reserve had completely deserted her. 'You mean she came to London? To see *you*?'

'And blind drunk with it,' Michael said. 'God knows how she did the drive.'

'Amazing,' Bron said, shaking his head. 'Amazing. Poor old Phil.'

'But what did she want? What did she expect *you* to do?'

'Nothing,' Michael said.

It was some time before Sophia would let him continue. She worried every detail, blamed herself, kept thinking of more traumas her mother must have suffered. She snapped at Bron, wept a little, stared at Michael as though the depths of his treachery made her feel faint. 'But she never said a word!' she kept repeating. 'I rang her only last week. She never said a word!'

'Anyway,' Michael said at last, rapping a baton. Sophia was silent. 'Anyway. I took her back, and I've been down quite often – spent a couple of weeks there in the summer, actually –'

'Why didn't you tell me?' Sophia stormed. 'Why didn't anybody tell me?'

'She thought you would be upset. She was worried about you, you know. You can't just go flitting off leaving your husband and kids on a whim –'

'Shut up, Mike,' Bron said amiably. 'How is she now?'

'That's why I came –'

'About time,' Sophia muttered, huddled.

'She's fine. She got together with Rebecca Broune's daughter, Isabel, and they spent a lot of time sight-seeing together. That seemed to do her good. But Isabel's got some sort of job here in London, and when I was down last weekend I had a feeling . . . I don't know. It's hard to explain. She won't

talk about the future. Everything else, but from tomorrow on
– nothing.'

This defeated Sophia. She frowned, blinked, trying to
understand. 'But she's not unhappy?'

'Just the opposite. She's never seemed happier. She's been
making her Will.'

'Oh God,' Sophia breathed slowly. 'You don't mean ...
You don't think ... Oh Mike – not *Mother* ...'

'She's not ill, as far as you know?' Bron asked.

'Sure of it. I just get this feeling that she's – well, packing
up. That she's got some crazy fantasy or other. She's not very
reliable.'

'Not reliable? Mother? I know she had a ghastly shock,
but –'

'I doubt whether she's ever been really reliable,' Michael
said. 'She's a – well, she's quite a skittish sort of woman
actually.'

'*Skittish?*' Sophia's beautiful mouth hung open; her beautiful eyes were wide with disbelief; she looked very much as
Selina looked when assailed by doubt as to the sanity of the
world.

'And obstinate. Whatever it is, she's not letting on. I think
she needs something practical to look forward to – some sort
of plan that'll bring her down to earth. Christmas, for example.'

'Christmas?'

'Supposing you all went to stay with her for Christmas.
Would that be possible?'

Sophia and Bron looked at each other. Sophia hunched her
shoulders, picked at a loose thread on her jeans.

'We'd hoped,' Bron said, 'to have Christmas here. Just the
four of us. But if she'd like to come, we'd of course –'

'She wouldn't,' Michael said. 'You can ask her if you like,
but I know she wouldn't. Anyway, it's not the point. The
point is to anchor her down there. Make her feel it's her home.
Give her a chance to get back to that endless cooking and

fussing. She'd decorate the place, get a tree, feel established. Surely you see what I mean?'

'What about you?' Sophia asked.

'I'll come if there's room, certainly. But it's your kids she needs. I don't think you realize how attached she is to Jasper.'

'Of course I do,' Sophia said uncomfortably. She sent a doleful message to Bron across the room. 'What do you think?'

'No question,' Bron said in the voice of a good loser. 'Of course we'll go. It'll be fun, Christmas in the country. Give her a ring, Sophia. Suggest it.'

'Now? But –'

'Yes, now.'

'But don't say I'm here,' Michael warned. 'Don't for God's sake say I've seen you even. It's entirely your own idea, understand?'

'But we're taking Jasper to Aladdin on Boxing Day, he's been looking forward to it –'

'Sophia,' Bron said. 'The telephone.'

She went to it as though it were a nasty mess. She wanted to howl with disappointment and guilt. The number rang for over a minute. 'She's not there,' Sophia said hopefully. Then, in her sepulchral telephone voice, 'Mother?'

*

'Christmas?' Phyllis said. 'Why, darling? I don't know. I hadn't thought. I don't ... Come *here*?' In a moment the dignified, paper-hatless, crackerless merriment of The Manor was forgotten; she was in a ferment of pudding and pies, turkey and cranberry jelly (no, redcurrant for Jasper), stockings and chimneys and holly and Noel, Noel. 'But of *course*! How *lovely*! But darling, it's so soon – only twenty more shopping days the paper says – there'll be such a lot to *do* ... No, no, of course I can, of course I can manage, good heavens, I've been doing Christmas since before you were born! I'd somehow thought you'd be wanting to stay at home this year

184

... Yes, of course it is ... Well, you'll probably see more of them than you would at home and I'm not going to have you washing up, Bron and I can do it, or Jasper and I for that matter ... Which day will you come? ... Yes, let me know. Perhaps Michael will come too. We'll be all together, won't that be fun? Will Jasper and Selina be all right in the attic? It's very warm, as you know ...' She saw a Christmas attic hung with streamers and stars, glimmering with fairy lights – no candles, of course. 'Thank you, Sophia ... Yes, I'm wonderfully well ... Thank you, darling.'

She was wreathed and spangled with smiles; she could feel them creeping about her face, dancing in front of her eyes, twinkling in her ears, sparkling on the hand she involuntarily raised to her mouth to check them. Everything had come right. Her soul magnified the lord and her spirit rejoiced. She would give Jasper a Christmas he would remember for the rest of his life; all his other Christmases would, by comparison, fall short of it. So much to do, so much to do. Good little house, she thought fondly, patting it. It would have its moment, its justification, after all. She might even ask Rebecca for drinks on Christmas morning, show her how real people live, proper people. Perhaps they would delay putting in the advertisement. No one would be buying property over Christmas, anyway. She must write to The Manor immediately, and say 17 January. Perhaps she would tell them all, once Christmas was over. They might see then that her mind was made up. The rest of her life stretched before her like a flowery meadow, an actual Paradise. How lucky I am. Thank you, God. Thank you, Gerald. And so much to do, good heavens, so much to be done.

She could have used Isabel's help now, but Isabel had gone. Never mind, she would take it slowly. It would have to be a bought pudding, but that couldn't be helped. She ordered the turkey – the butcher was getting quite friendly now, since Michael had been there so often – and made the brandy butter, a grimace at the smell of the stuff, how she had ever drunk it she couldn't think. She went back to Mr Weaver for her tree, so full of sprightly goodwill that he realized she hadn't found out about the fence posts and helped her select a real beauty, with a pot to put it in. He would lift it himself, he said, and deliver it on the Thursday so that she could get it decorated in good time. He was pleased to hear she hadn't had any more trouble with Brigadier Wainwright. Turning the other cheek had certainly paid off in that case, he said.

Always smiling, always on her toes, she scoured the surrounding towns and markets for baubles and toys, mistletoe and glitter, robins and paper lace, angels and holly. Putting off taking it all to the attic, she hoarded it in the kitchen, such a pile that she couldn't for the life of her remember what was what. At night, while watching television, she made paper chains – hideous things, but the children would like them. She bought, as well as bird-watching equipment for Jasper, a bird table, a nesting box, and nuts in a mesh container. Jasper could have them all next year – she thought they probably already had such things at The Manor, because they would be of great interest to the old people. She thought of herself as a very junior member of The Manor. It made her feel like a girl again. Dear old things, if only they could see her now.

Christmas Day was on Saturday. Michael would come for the night – he could sleep on the floor in the attic, he said he was quite used to that – and Jasper and the family would stay until the end of the week. Phyllis put aside the last Sunday for decorating the attic, since she couldn't go shopping. Then there would be nothing left but the tree, of course they would all help with that, a bottle of champagne and Pepsi-Cola for Jasper, not normally allowed. There was frosty sunlight streaming through the attic window, seasonal music on the radio, she toiled up the narrow stairs with armfuls of gifts and frippery, came down sideways for another load, tidings of comfort and joy and a short rest for soup, now for the last two carrier bags and the paper chains.

She always remembered to shut the stairs door because of

the draught, though it wasn't easy with your hands full in that confined space. A pity she hadn't managed to do anything about the draughts, or the wretched door for that matter – whoever bought the cottage would undoubtedly deal with them. She crept up, step by step, peering over the heap of coloured paper towards the sunlight on the landing. When she reached it, she realized she had forgotten the Bluetack. Oh dear, what a nuisance. She dropped the load of carrier bags and paper chains on the floor and turned to hurry back down the stairs, her hand now free to grasp the rope bannister. She slipped on the second stair; for a dizzy moment she swung by the rope; the frayed strands broke against her weight and she dived into the black well of the staircase, the firmly shut door meeting her head on.

*

The radio played until midnight, then switched to a high-pitched hum like the vibration of stars. The Brig Boys, seeing the old bag's light on at two in the morning, whooped and cat-called. The village heard them in several dreams, thought nothing of it. At six o'clock, in the dark, Phyllis's radio said good morning.

The postman left a bill and what looked like a couple of Christmas cards. Some members of the local Hunt clopped by, distantly elevated, looking neither to right nor left. Bill Slattery sat by the range reading the racing results.

On Tuesday there were three more cards; on Wednesday a mail order catalogue, hardly worth forcing through the letter box. The postman went away whistling 'Rudolf the Red-Nosed Reindeer', which was playing on the radio at the time.

Rebecca was preparing to hibernate through the cruel months. A few last drops of life smeared the pages of her notebook. Winter silence had already closed in over the disturbance of birds and insects. The sound of the telephone startled her.

'It's Michael Muspratt. I've been trying to get hold of my

mother. I've been ringing her since Sunday but there's no reply, and my sister tried yesterday – anyway, I'm a bit worried. Could you go up and see if she's all right?'

'I suppose so,' Rebecca said.

'We're all coming down on Friday – she's probably just busy, out somewhere, but I'd be most grateful –'

'Your concern is very touching,' Rebecca said, thinking how he had nearly killed her. 'Do you want me to ring you?'

'If you would. I'm at the office – I'll give you the number.'

'I have the number,' she said, and rang off.

The last thing she wanted was a chat with the little Muspratt, dizzy with the Christmas spirit. However, there was nothing for it. She heaved herself into her jacket, pocketed her cigarettes and set off up the hill.

Seeing a light on and hearing the wireless, she was tempted to slink away. She knocked once more, looking with disgust at the balled roses dead on their stems, the soggy lambs' ears and sprawled lavender. She peered through the kitchen window – not quite tidy enough for the little Muspratt, but nothing outrageous. Perhaps for some absurd reason she was in the garden, or pottering about at the back. She went round the house, hesitated, tried the back door. Finding it unlocked – surprising, surely it would be natural to Phyllis to lock up at all times – she stepped cautiously into the kitchen. A woman was flutingly reading some abominable short story – ' "This business about people passing like ships in the night is all wrong," he said . . .' Impatiently, with something like a small jab of fear, she turned the radio off. Silence rushed in. There was a dirty mug on the table, a litter of scissors and glue. The post was still on the floor. 'Mrs Muspratt?' she called. 'Mrs Muspratt? Are you there?' She had to wrestle with the stairs door, finally opened it. Phyllis tumbled at her feet, a small heap of cloth and hair and petrified body. A drift of paper chains, lifted on the draught, blew gently down the stairs and settled over her legs, a gaudy covering.

25

The regulation of death began. Dr Martin, who had seen many smashed skulls on the hunting field, rang up his friend Harry Barnes, the coroner. Not a chance, he said, must have gone out like a light. Pity she hadn't been found sooner, but it wouldn't have made a jot of difference. Thanks, Harry, see you on Boxing Day.

'When her son arrives,' he said, scribbling, 'give him this and see he takes it to the registrar – I've put the address here – Jim Stevenson, nice fellow. He'll give him the disposal certificate and all that bumpf. You don't happen to know whether she'll be cremated?'

'How would I know?' Rebecca asked.

'No. Well. Get her son – what's his name? Muspratt? – to give me a ring. He'd better get on to the undertakers as soon as possible – Co-op's as good as any, they'll come out right away. You can stay till he gets here, can you? No point in me hanging about.' He loomed in the winter afternoon, his face like a sun in fog. 'Any problems?'

Rebecca said nothing. He had covered the little Muspratt with a blanket. Rebecca sat alone in the room, waiting.

When Michael arrived he seemed frozen, walked stiffly, hardly moved his lips as he spoke. He went over to the mound of his mother, raised the corner of the blanket, dropped it again. He telephoned the undertaker. Rebecca didn't know whether to leave or stay. He didn't seem to expect either, so she stayed. He asked only two questions.

'Did the doctor say – how long?'

'Three days. Since Sunday.'

'Did he know whether it was – was she killed outright?'

'He said so.'

They separated into their own fearful thoughts. The undertakers arrived, Mr Watts and Mr Bridewell. A younger man lurked in the front garden with a stretcher. Mr Bridewell seemed to be in charge. He was a portly man and spoke in a soft, high voice, like a child stroking a kitten. 'I shall be dealing with things for you,' he said. 'We shall see to the first offices, of course. Would you care for a shroud or a robe? Or perhaps your mother had a favourite nightgown?'

'I don't care,' Michael said. 'Take her away.'

'It's the shock,' Mr Bridewell said to Rebecca, excusing him. 'I'll just leave our little brochure here,' he placed it reverently on the table, 'and you can look at it at your leisure.' He raised his voice slightly to address Michael. 'I will telephone you tomorrow morning, sir,' then, sotto voce to Rebecca, 'Perhaps you would both care to leave the room while we remove the deceased?'

There was nowhere else to go. The younger man came in with a folding stretcher, like a beach chair. They bundled Phyllis on to it, blanket and all, and covered it up. In order to get it to the front door they had to move the wingchair and table. 'We'll just pop her in the handy,' Mr Bridewell whispered, 'and I'll come back and tidy up.' He was almost conspiratorial with Rebecca, who may have appeared not to be grieving. When he had straightened the chair and table and said a meaningful good night to Michael, he beckoned Rebecca outside.

'It's most unfortunate that there was such … unavoidable delay. The post mortem staining, you understand, is very –'

'I've seen her,' Rebecca said, and left him.

'You can spend the night with me, if you like,' she said to Michael.

He looked at her vaguely.

'Well – come down any time. The door's open,' she said, and left him too.

*

From the devastated household in London there came a soft, constant wail of if only, the west wind of death. If only we hadn't interfered ... if only we'd known ... if only she could have got to the phone ... if only someone had seen to that rope, that door ... if only she'd waited until we came ... if only ... if only ... There was no point in them coming until the funeral. Cremation? If only she could be buried, properly, in a churchyard ... if only she'd talked about it, if only they had known. It was like holding a shell to one's ear; put it down, smother it, refuse to listen, but the desolate moan went on.

Michael stayed at the cottage. Mr Bridewell rang up. It all depended, of course, what one's views were. In his own, cremation was by far the best, particularly in a case like this. Burial, he admitted, was simpler in some ways – not so much red tape, and possibly a little cheaper, depending on the coffin and the kind of ceremony required. But the cemetery was – well, he wouldn't want his own mother buried there, should he put it like that. Graves required constant attention, and all too often ... frankly, in his view, the cemetery was nothing more than a wilderness. Now with cremation you had a number of choices – there was the Book of Memory, £8.91 for a two-line inscription inclusive of V A T, or he could have Mrs Muspratt's name inscribed on a Recordia Panel, though he wasn't sure whether they had any room left for December entries. Or a bronze Memorial Plaque, what about that? A really beautiful job, right there in the Garden of Remembrance, £55.20 – including V A T as before – really a joy for ever, though of course the Corporation had the right to remove it after twenty years. No upkeep with cremation, no guilt – he had known families quite worn down with guilt over Grandma's grave – and above all hygienic. If Mrs Muspratt hadn't expressed any views on the matter, Mr Bridewell would strongly advise cremation.

Michael listened attentively, but didn't hear. He remembered his father as an effigy; his mother had for the present become diseased, a gaping mouth with no scream, staring eyes with none of the liveliness of terror. He wanted to shout burn her, burn her, while tenderness and pity disabled him. 'Hang on a minute,' he said. 'There's someone at the door.'

A fellow with a Christmas tree. 'She's dead,' Michael said. 'Take it away.'

'But it's paid for –'

'Give it to someone. Take it away.'

Cremation, on the other hand, Mr Bridewell continued smoothly, did necessitate a certain amount of paper work. There was Form A, the application, which would have to be countersigned by a householder who had known Mrs Muspratt personally; then there were Forms B, C and F. Form C must be completed by a different doctor from the doctor who completed Form B, and Form F must be completed by a different doctor entirely. Mr Bridewell knew it sounded a little complicated, but it was just a matter of – well, a matter of form you might say, with no smile in his voice.

'What about D and E?' Michael asked.

'There is no Form D or Form E.'

Had she gone through all this with his father? If not, who had? The bureaucracy of death amazed him. Forty-four years old, and he had thought it as simple as throwing a dead bird on a bonfire. 'There's someone at the door again. Could I ring you back?'

'Certainly,' Mr Bridewell said. 'Bereavement is always a busy time.'

A very young parson and his obvious wife; trim dog-collar above a cricket or rowing sweater, grey flannels not seen by Michael for ten years, the ubiquitous khaki parka; a slab of hair continually pushed back and falling across eager eyes. 'I'm Brian Philipps – Vicar of Lamberts Heath – we just heard the tragic news and we – Pat and I, this is my wife Pat – we felt we should come and offer our sincere, our very sincere sympathy. You *are* Mr Muspratt?'

'Did you know my mother?' Michael asked.

'No – unfortunately no – I think she was perhaps not a

regular church-goer – however of course that makes no difference to our – it's indeed a terrible thing, I believe she wasn't found for several days?'

There was something about sparrows stored in Michael's memory since school Sundays; insignificant birds, but not one of them fell to the ground without God's knowledge. Since he couldn't quote it correctly, or with the bitterness he felt, he kept quiet.

'Perhaps you would like to talk about the arrangements?' the Vicar said helplessly, glancing at Pat for strength. They were not going to be asked in. 'As a parishioner, your mother is of course entitled – I assume she was Church of England? Not Catholic, by any chance?'

'No,' Michael said.

'Ah. Well. The churchyard here is hardly practical, I'm afraid, but there's a charming cemetery in Lamberts Heath – jolly nice, isn't it, Pat? – if you'd like to consider that – and of course I'd be happy, most happy, to conduct –'

'How much?'

'I'm sorry – I – ? Ah. How much. Well, of course that depends whether you would like a church service beforehand and the type of – grave you require.'

'She'll be cremated,' Michael said.

'Cremated. Yes, I see. Well in that case – there's a jolly nice chapel at the crematorium, if you would like me to –'

'No, thanks,' Michael said. He closed the door and watched them going down the path, Pat holding the Vicar's arm and perhaps comforting him. Where shall we put you, what shall we do with you? He rang Mr Bridewell. He tried to understand. 'Sorry,' he said. 'The door again.' Mr Bridewell's voice stepped back into the shadows, prepared to wait.

A savage young woman with protruding teeth. 'The *Western Daily Echo*. I understand that someone fell down the stairs and wasn't found for four days, is that so?'

Michael shut the door. He picked up the receiver. 'All right,' he said. 'What do I do now?'

*

Phyllis's body spent Christmas in the cold room at the mortuary, the crematorium being closed for business over the season of goodwill. Mr Bridewell arranged the cremation for what he called the Tuesday, distinguishing it from any other Tuesday in Phyllis's life. He was used to his clients veering from intense interest – privately he considered it interference – to abject helplessness. Michael was more interested and more helpless than most. Mr Bridewell steered him in the direction of ultimate indifference, which he himself had reached long ago.

Isabel arrived, completely silent at first, shadowing furniture with her presence, slipping through half-closed doors. Michael, worn out, turned up at Rebecca's on Christmas Eve. 'I'd thought of going back to London, but I might as well stay, if that's all right.'

'That's all right,' Rebecca said. The Christmas Oratorio filled the house, but it was impossible to tell which of the three, if any, were listening. None of them spoke anything but their most simple thoughts. They might have been people at the end of a very long journey, or idiots.

Phyllis's Will, awaiting the completion of her arrangements at The Manor, had never been finished. There was a note written on Michael's writing paper clipped to the draft. 'Until further arrangements M. & B. execs & everything to them for sale not to Brig. – or deal with as they think best. No flowers.' If only she'd gone to The Manor for Christmas as she'd planned, if only there could be a few flowers. Regret sighed constantly through Rebecca's telephone. It was the worst Christmas Jasper could remember.

The Tuesday, as Mr Bridewell had planned, was at least sunny; it was even warm, a mock spring in the Garden of Remembrance. Michael, Isabel and Rebecca went to the crematorium in one of Mr Bridewell's cars, a doleful vehicle slowly driven by last Wednesday's stretcher-bearer. Sophia, Bron and Jasper were already there. Sophia had seldom stopped crying since she had heard of her mother's death. She had cried so much that she was thin, and bruised round the eyes. She wore her usual sombre clothes, which seemed too big for her. Bron never let go of Jasper's hand. He felt over-poweringly guilty, as though he had been part of a conspiracy to maim and finally murder his mother-in-law. Even Jasper, at six years old, must be controlled.

Mr Bridewell and Mr Watts stood by the hearse, frequently looking at their watches. Mr Bridewell suggested that Mr Muspratt's party should wait in the room designed for that purpose – a waiting room with nothing on the grey walls but a No Smoking sign, Rexine benches in front of small hex-agonal tables there for no reason but to display a few dog-eared numbers of *Woman and Home*. Rebecca went outside, smoking her way past the Hybrid Teas and Floribundas. Bron and Jasper waited in the car. Presumably Michael and Sophia stayed with Isabel indoors.

A group of people shuffled out of the chapel and stood about uncertainly until they were marshalled by their funeral director into a waiting convoy. By the time they had gone, Phyllis's hearse was empty. Fred Skerry's car cruised up the drive and swung into the car park. Rebecca joined the family in the chapel.

There was the usual kind of music on tape: it might have been recorded for going up and down in the lift of a tower or spire. There was no service. They sat hearing the tape, their eyes on the small, bare coffin. Jasper fidgeted a bit. Sophia sobbed desolately. Michael stood up, said, 'Well, we all knew her,' and sat down again. The curtains slowly closed, hiding the coffin. The performance was over.

Fred stood at the back of the chapel in a grave attitude. The family, not knowing him, filed past him and out of the door.

'Well, Fred.'

'Well, Rebecca. I thought you'd be here. I read it in the paper. Terrible thing. Terrible.'

'Yes.'

'No flowers, I see. That's a shame. I could have brought a few chrysanths. I never think it's a proper job without flowers.' He smiled solemnly. 'I'll call by one day. It's been a long time.'

Rebecca said, 'It was a question of the draughts, I believe. And the rope. And the door.'

'Yes. I'm afraid I never got around to those. Pity.'

The car was waiting. Rebecca climbed in, and they drove away.

*

They went back to Coachman's Cottage. Isabel, apparently, had tidied it and provided food of a sort. There was champagne and, for Jasper, Pepsi-Cola. Except for Jasper none of them ate or drank. Sophia drifted about aimlessly, picking up small objects. She went upstairs and came back shaking. Bron took Jasper up to the attic. He climbed down carefully – Bron hovered – clasping two bulging Christmas stockings. Then he found the bird table and the nesting box out in the yard. Michael said he could have them. Everyone felt better for a few minutes, but bewilderment soon returned.

'We must go,' Bron said. 'We've left Selina.' He shook Michael's hand, insisting that he was available at any time. He shook Rebecca's hand and thanked her. He shook hands with Isabel, thanking her too. Jasper marched out with his loot, but Sophia faded gradually after hugging her brother and weeping into his shirt; she didn't know who Rebecca and Isabel were and would never remember them as anything but unknown mourners. Knowing that she loved her husband and son, she followed them; there was nowhere else to go.

Isabel said she would stay and clear up. Michael offered to help her. From this moment their futures were of no concern to Rebecca. She urgently wanted to be alone. That in no way describes the urgency of her need. Hands in her pockets, she lumbered down the path. The Brigadier's car – a big, dull Humber, he'd had it for twenty years – drew up as she went through the gate. She was trapped by it.

'Ah. Mrs Broune.'

He was sitting in the back with two of his men; another three in front, quite a posse. The aides tipped their tweed hats. They looked uncomfortable.

'Is Mr Muspratt at home?' Wainwright asked.

She didn't answer.

'Captain Foster?'

The driver opened his door. Rebecca slammed it on him.

'Get out!' she yelled. 'You bastards! Get out of here!'

She had no idea what she would do if they refused. Fight, she supposed. The aides glanced uncertainly at Wainwright. What a pathetic lot they were. Their moustaches were nibbled; they had old, trembling hands; they weren't going to last much longer.

'You should be ashamed of yourselves,' Rebecca said gently.

They cowered, muttering to Wainwright. He hesitated, then nodded at the driver. The car lurched off up the hill, putting on speed as it turned the corner.

Rebecca waited until it had gone, then walked home dragging her feet, slower and slower until she got to the gate. She opened it, shut it, went into her garden. Cut back the ramblers. She saw herself in gloves, with secateurs, cutting back the ramblers.

'Wish I could wear gloves.'

'Why can't you?'

She could, of course.

A winter afternoon. Not yet the black and iron of winter, though. A dazzling sky, gold as charity, burnished for the little Muspratt up in heaven. Jesus. Christ Jesus, what an end. She opened the work-room door. Triumphant light through the west window gilding the mess. Secateurs there, and gloves.

She sat down on the packing case. Nauseated. Blood boiling in her neck and face, jolting through her veins. A sense of wonder and reluctance. Dread. Godawful dread in her stomach.

She sat without moving for some time, then slowly swivelled round to face the window. Looking out at the valley, not moving her eyes, she shifted string and wire, dropped a couple of seed trays on the floor, cleared a space. Holding the valley in her eyes, the shine and the dark, she fitted paper into the typewriter, turned the platten knob, checked the spacing. Then, fingers lying over the keys, she waited.

Gerald walked to the french windows in the dining room. His jacket hung loose from his shoulder blades, the back of his head was buff and straggly. Not an old man, but about to die.

A memorial, then, to both of them, extinct as they are, foolish, fond, courageous and insignificant.

Rebecca wrote down words, her roses dormant, the little Muspratt a carton of ash scattered in a garden locked at sunset. Which soon, unnoticed by any of them, it was.